My Plan to Have an Office

Chun-Te Liao

authorHOUSE®

AuthorHouse™ UK
1663 Liberty Drive
Bloomington, IN 47403 USA
www.authorhouse.co.uk
Phone: 0800 047 8203 (Domestic TFN)
+44 1908 723714 (International)

Published by AuthorHouse 08/22/2019

ISBN: 978-1-7283-9206-6 (sc)
ISBN: 978-1-7283-9207-3 (hc)
ISBN: 978-1-7283-9205-9 (e)

Preface

My Plan to Have an Office is a fiction novel that tells the story of a translator commissioned by a publishing house. He has just taken over a studio and has translated a novel called *Summer Capriccio*.

This novel contains some opera-related discussions because one of the characters is an opera lover.

The operas mentioned in the story are as follows:

1. *Ernani* by Verdi
2. *Andrea Chenier* by Giordano
3. *Fedora* by Giordano
4. *Manon Lescaut* by Puccini

A musical recording cannot be expressed in words, but in the novel, it is shared by mentioning the tracks. This is the difference between words and music. I hope you have time to listen to and enjoy these beautiful opera selections and songs.

I once had the idea of writing a sequel to this book, but perhaps the difficulty with writing a second book is how to attract readers' interest at the beginning of the story. And I am still thinking about the different operatic discussions and fresh content from the first book.

Perhaps there are still many things that need answers in this story. However, through one chapter after another, things are gradually resolved. The truth of the facts may be in the text of the book. The truth is revealed between the lines.

In the story, the protagonist finds some old opera-related articles, dating back to the Italian Naples in 1835, and later, he reads the work log of the former studio director that gave him a deeper understanding and inspiration for the work of this studio.

The protagonist is a brave and independent spirit, like an adult in a postmodern age, but he also dreams of home. He eager to return to his home one day, but in the meantime, his work has enriched his life. At the same time, he feels homesick, and that feelings increases day by day.

Chapter 1

wo years have passed since I said farewell to my former work environment, and time has passed very fast. Maybe I never really left that city. I still see some old friends on Facebook, where they share their lives and their current situations. Most of them post content that is nothing more than talking about the party in the restaurant or activities at the club or photos of their overseas travel. It seems like I'm reading newspapers or watching the TV news. Generally speaking, I don't really understand why some people have to share about what they've been doing recently.

My friendship with them has not been continued. I know that their current situations will maintain the illusion that all is well with them; it's a very familiar dynamic of theirs. But in reality, it is like they are strangers or in a strange and unfamiliar dilemma. I gradually came to realize that what I knew about them was just the former them or the former working environment of theirs, instead of the persons they portray on Facebook, meeting with others, having group activities with others, or just being with others. They don't include me. If they are traveling abroad together, I am not a friend that they know. Why do I have to see photos of their gatherings with others?

Why? I thought that we'd lost contact, but I often see their news. Facebook still regards us as a group of friends who have an interaction. This is a new definition of friends—a group relationship that will exist in the online world of modern people. Is it that after another generation, I won't have to explain this relationship to myself or to others?

Today, when I met my colleague, I told him about the upcoming copies of the book I wrote. It's the story of a single man and woman; it's their love story.

There are new photos on Facebook. I have seen many examples of "star faces" that gave the illusion, in that group photo, that I know who certain of them are, yet certain of them I do not know. I have to distinguish between them; it becomes a thing that needs to be identified. Otherwise, I will get the wrong impression of them.

Meanwhile, I am meeting with other friends for afternoon tea. When I talked to myself, practicing my conversations with them, I accidentally said, "It seems that you are very prosperous." What should I do? Rationality says to be myself, but that might gradually alienate them—alienate friends who recognize my face. From being nodding acquaintances to becoming friends, then becoming friends who "like" each other on Facebook, and then becoming strangers. Finally, one day, I thought, Who are they? So I deleted them.

Despite this, my life has not been calm; it is a hotbed, raising my fertile and rich sounds, infiltrating me with a spirit. For a moment, everyone has become like that, and there is no problem with our relationships.

I'm now living in a big city. It's so convenient here—it's easy to shop with one hand; it's easy to satisfy myself, and it's easy to become a worm.

Good transportation here—the subway and road traffic every day and streets that seem to extend in all directions. With the underground and skyscrapers, it is still a 3-D city. No wonder I am unfamiliar here. We only listen to public radio stations, and we do not call each other!

It is also very fashionable here. Many advertisements, magazines, and department stores introduce famous-brand products. Postmodernism advocates a simple style—the simpler and the less material, the more fashionable.

It's so casual here. There are many coffeehouses, cafés, and steakhouses, and they are open late to provide office workers, student crowds, and many vacationers with a place to get a bite to eat, a drink, or just to socialize. I need three weeks in advance to make a reservation in a café or to find the location of the restaurant. There are always crowds, and I'm lazy. How can I find a quiet, laid-back restaurant with delicious food?

This is the living environment of this metropolitan city. I know that some people must travel because of their work. So several important big cities, such as Paris, Rome, Shanghai, New York, and London, are connected. It's like a regional network.

During the summer vacation, many people go abroad. Some of them go to Japan; Thailand; Guangzhou, China; or Moscow. They all reported their vacations on Facebook, and they were envied by others. I am not in contact with them. Were they you on the road? On a business trip? Or was this their last vacation in summer?

This song comes from a webcast:

> I miss you.
> I still miss you.
> Everything has no end.
> Until I look forward to it,
> I believe that love has gone far.

Let's bless and be there for each other. Be brave enough to live!

Chapter 2

*I*f I could predict my future, then what do I urgently need to do and what goals must I achieve?

A mastermind of development said, "If you want to achieve new goals, see yourself as already having achieved them."

I look at my appearance in the mirror. I look unobtrusive. I have a medium build, short black hair, a long oval face, plump lips, and a big nose, and I'm wearing black-rimmed eyeglasses. Sometimes I look at the mirror for a long time, and I think, *Is that me?*

Then I answer myself: *The new year is here. What do you expect to look like?*

Should I be slimmer and not have too much fat on my body? Should I change my hairstyle or dye my hair? Should I consider joining a gym or health club where I can cycle or take an aerobics course?

If I could change only a small part of me, maybe this year's change will be very limited, not like some of the shocking movies I've seen or novels I've read. I think, *I have to determine my own center first, not just count on creativity.*

Now, I am in my office, surveying this writing studio that I just took over. My purpose for taking over the studio was to give me a place to do some professional writing. I need to write an article based on human nature—on humanity—as well as the lifestyle in SoHo's, and I need to create a personal brand image.

The content of my writing will include:

1. an opera thesis,
2. special articles,
3. mood-focused prose, and
4. short stories and novels.

Looking over this studio, I've found plans, proposals, books, and recordings, which will let me do some retrospectives.

In terms of planning, I want to establish the Opera Music and Education Foundation. I will do this according to the "Principles of Foundation Establishment"; there is a so-called building fund that's worth about one hundred thousand dollars.

The hardware of the plan is as follows:

*   desktop LCD monitor and computer
*   computer desk
*   LCD TV
*   notebook computer
*   two iPad minis, equipped with company mobile phone
*   iPhone
*   printer
*   desk
*   four briefcases—one for folders, one for business cards, one for a backpack, and one for a tote.

In terms of furniture, the studio contains the following:

*   desk (writing desk)
*   loveseat
*   table lamp
*   antique hanging wall clock
*   wooden liquor cabinet
*   aromatherapy steam machine
*   air-conditioning unit
*   electric piano

Also as part of the deal, I got a white four-passenger car.

The 3C (computer, communication, and consumer electronics) products, supplies, and everything else are all being looked after. Due to the cost of establishing the studio, it is currently only possible for me to rent a house and a rental office in the Metropolitan Business Center, with a monthly rent of about two thousand dollars.

Before I moved into the studio, I sorted through all the proposals, materials, and recordings that had been left behind. I found the following:

1. The *My Opera Experience* anthology—the official version has been published, and the English version is still being organized.
2. Some travel records; for example, Italy: the south of Italy, the cities of Salerno and Rome.
3. Proposals for the publication of books: *My New Year's Life Proposal, Travel around Roma, and Speak Italian,* and *The First Approach to a Legend Novel.*

Among them, *My New Year's Life Proposal* is the author's description of the changes that take place in postmodern life and habits, as opposed to the current living conditions and the precautions we should take in the face of "old age."

Travel around Roma, and Speak Italian is a story-based travelogue that combines sightseeing photos with simple, primary Italian-language lessons.

And *The First Approach to Legend Novel* is defined as a biographical novel, but the content was partly lost—for unspecified reasons.

Other finds included a screenplay, which is supposed to be a movie made from an original novel and a proposal to adapt the script, but it has not been completed. And there is also a proposal to work with the opera music magazine, which seems to be a partnership with tacit understanding.

With regard to this studio, I immediately realized I needed help. I still hope to find someone who can be trusted, because I need someone to help me with these unfinished proposals. I need to finish these efforts started by the members of the studio a long time ago.

In terms of recording materials, I've found a number of songs and have inquired about the tracks.

Part 1—Songs

1. Caccini—"Amarilli"
2. Scarlatti—"O cessate di piagarmi"
3. Handel—"Lascia ch'io pianga"
4. Martini—"Piacer d'amor"
5. Giordani—"Caro mio ben"
6. Bellini—"Vaga luna che inargenti"
7. Verdi—"In solitaria stanza"
8. Leoncavallo—"Mattinata"
9. Handel—"V'adoro, pupille"
10. Handel—"Tornami a vagheggiar"
11. Tosti—"La serenata"

Part 2—Arias

1. *La Traviata*—"Un di felice eterea"
2. *La Traviata*—"Lunge da lei, per me"
3. *La Traviata*—"Parigi, o, cara"
4. *Rigoletto*—"Questa o quella"
5. *Rigoletto*—"E sol dell'anima"
6. *Rigoletto*—"Ella mi fu rapita"
7. *Rigoletto*—"Parmi veder le lagrime"
8. *Lucia di Lammermoor*—"Tombe degli avi miei"
9. *Lucia di Lammermoor*—"Fra poco a me ricovero"
10. *Lucia di Lammermoor*—"Tu che a Dio spiegasti l'ali"

With the above recordings, I speculate that it may be a test for a planned studio recording. I have heard that the former studio director likes opera very much and occasionally sings one or two lines of lyrics. He might even be planning to go to Italy to practice vocal music.

In terms of a work schedule with the publisher and the publishing house in New York, I know so little about them, but I need to immediately start working, translating manuscripts into English and looking for a closer publisher. I only know of one publishing house that will accept email submissions.

I am still praying in my heart that a trustworthy person will appear to help me. I will accomplish this step by step and succeed with my plan. I wonder how important and meaningful is it to the members of the studio.?

Chapter 3

I saw a comment on the Internet today: "Missing someone is even more terrible than the impact of death."

However, what I thought was, *Becoming old is more terrible than missing anyone.*

As time has gone by, I quickly have stepped into the age of no doubt—forty—reminding me that I cannot relax and that everything should be carried out according to the proposal put forward for the studio. Unless there is an irresistible power against my reaching the goal, I swear not to give up.

Finally, after several days, the English version of *Summer Dreams* was submitted by email to the American Publishing House in New York, together with an introductory letter. A total of five e-mails have now been exchanged—it's nine o'clock in the evening, but New York may be nearer to nine o'clock in the morning.

The next proposal is *Travel around Roma, and Speak Italian.* I searched the internet, Google, Amazon, and other webpages. There are no related books.

I have reviewed again the purpose of this studio. This studio has four components, which are composed of these four parts:

1. company
2. studio
3. writing room
4. Opera Music and Education Foundation

The proportion of each of them has yet to be determined, but in a word, the idea is that a studio based on the name of the foundation and the establishment of the foundation must be carried out in accordance with the "Principles of Foundation Establishment" regulations. There are problems with the preparation of the construction fund, so that part is still hard at work, but what is certain is this: there will be an opera music commemorative foundation known as the Opera Music and Education Foundation.

Therefore, it is more likely I will implement a method from the establishment of a writing room.

I think that the person in charge of the previous writing room may have been running a studio of this nature for five years. As I have just taken over, I want to introduce myself: I am an opera lover but I graduated from college with a degree in foreign languages, and because of the work of this studio, I still practice Italian. I just want to write some articles about opera music because I am a fan of opera. I have nearly a thousand music CDs, dozens of opera DVDs, and dozens of books related to opera music. I feel that I can no longer satisfy my love of opera with a mere listening experience. I not only listen but also have started to learn the language, and even try to write relevant articles. All of this is due to my love of opera.

Chapter 4

Talk from the Recent Replay of Verdi's Ernani *in Milan*

ecently it was shared by the La Scala Theater's account on Facebook that La Scala in Milan was about to stage the opera master Verdi's opera *Ernani*. As for Verdi's work, its popularity may not be as great as *Aida*, which is playing at the Metropolitan Opera in New York and is a big show, but *Ernani* has been performed by the "Iron Triangle" since 1982 at La Scala Opera House. Placido Domingo plays Ernani, Mirella Freni plays Elvira, and Nicolai Ghiaurov plays Don Ruy. This love-triangle relationship is like the other opera, *Il Trovatore*, but *Ernani* pays more attention to the dramatic improvisation of music, and includes the baritone role of Don Carlo. Therefore, the complexity of the plot increases. Don Ruy is convinced that Ernani and Elvira are together and thinks, *Lovers get married*. Meanwhile, a horn sounds in the distance. Ernani promised Don Ruy that if he ever felt that Ernani posed a threat to the entire empire, Don Ruy would only need to blow the horn, and after Ernani heard the horn, he would smack himself.

The cast and the version performed at La Scala Opera House in 1982 may still be the most classic version, with a full-length video version. The two roles of Verdi's male tenor and heroine soprano, Ernani and Elvira, are extremely difficult to perform. From the first-scene entrance, the tenor and the choir, led by the leading actor, followed the aria of the protagonist soprano and the horse song. Placido Domingo and Mirella Freni were the performers who interpreted Verdi at the time.

In particular, in 1979, Freni completed the full-length opera recording of *Aida* with the conductor Maestro Herbert von Karajan. It seems that the opera world also thinks of Italian soprano Signora Mirella Freni as the heroine in *Aida* in this opera. After this role, there is no soprano character that she is not capable of performing. And Freni even sang this role in the selection of Verdi's and Puccini's arias published in collaboration with Grammophon in 1994. This album is said to have broken the personal taboos of Mirella Freni, who did not sing Verdi's heroine Amelia in the "Un Ballo in Maschera." Since then, Verdi's dramatic interpretation by Signora Freni has been unquestionable. Some of her opera fans and lovers have even called her the "Freni phenomenon," which is from her early lyrical interpretation, with dramatic changes in the middle and later stages of her career.

As far as the opera *Ernani* is concerned, the emphasis on the grand arranging and the dramatic long treble for a general soprano—and how to achieve the effect of interpretation through the development of sound—is waiting to be seen. Otherwise, as far as Verdi's music is concerned, how a tenor can achieve that kind of heroic sound effect is what real opera fans expect. As for vocal skills, the male protagonist, Ernani, forces a general tenor to develop a transitional sound, using chest sounds or the sounds on the lower half of the register, as well as the high-pitched area. For the hero tenor, perhaps this is a difference in his choice of a Mozart, Richard Strauss, or Verdi tenor.

However, music has its own appeal, and the so-called beautiful singing—*bel canto*—is also indispensable. In order to pursue the opera role of a certain composer, it should not be thought that the vocal skills of the so-called bel canto method could be abandoned.

As for opera appreciation, Verdi's baritone and bass characters also have many moving and unique features. The most classic baritone character is the role of Rigoletto in the opera of the same name. For this play, Rigoletto is only a courtier and a jester, and Verdi's work shows a father's love for his daughter, Gilda. From this point of view of the plot, the baritone role of Rigoletto becomes flesh and blood. And it is similar to the role of Don Ruy in the opera *Ernani*, which in Verdi's work presents a male character with male righteousness.

The climax of *Ernani* is that Ernani heard the horn honking from afar, and he needed to respond to show his male loyalty and self-decision. The loyalty and heroism between men is also the essence of the work by Verdi. One of the features of his work is that there are so many connections to heroism. Some opera fans even call Verdi a "patriotic composer," which is full of chivalrous feelings.

La Scala's rehearsal of *Ernani*, for the postmodern period, nearly two decades after the millennium—what impact is brought about by this opera?

Chapter 5

Sharing My Opera Experience

*A*nother article I wrote was on the opera-viewing habits of postmodern people:

Because of my work, I have spent a lot of time on computers, mobile phones, or other 3C (computer, communication, and consumer electronics) products. When it comes to internet video, I find the viewing time too long. I've watched some movies, miniseries, and short videos, especially my favorite TV series, or I've listened to the recordings. Sometimes when it's a long play, I have to find some way to see it, other than to watch and listen to operas—the dramas based on music—one after another.

When operas were created, there was no TV; they were performed and staged in the theater. The staging, such as the background scenery, the protagonist's entrance, the length of the scene, and the structural integrity of the designs, make the drama unique. A drama is divided into several scenes and three, four, or five acts.

Because of the total length of the viewing time, from the curtain's rise to the final curtain and with the main theme of a scene combining with the theme of a play, it is necessary to consider streamlining for economic benefits, highlighting the climax of the plot and showing the skill of a great composer.

From the opera composers of the *bel canto*, such as Bellini and Donizetti, to the later composers, such as Verdi and Puccini, with their well-known dramas, all show the above characteristics. If one production and performance of the opera has mastered such principles, and the viewers can feel that the plot is compact, the rhythm is bright, then opera is worthy of the things that are sure to be loved by the audience.

So, do viewers who watch the video of an opera know that?

You may wonder how I choose the way to watch a play.

Thanks to modern technology, I can see an opera at a glance on YouTube, as well as being given information about it. For example, I can learn how old the opera is or who other famous composers were in the baroque period, or how long the opera is. For example, Handel's opera runs for more than three hours. If I were not a fan of this opera, how could I spend more than three hours doing nothing else but concentrating on watching the drama?

I think that opera fans can understand that I love to watch the play of an opera, and I want to sit still for it. I can watch for such a long time because of the beauty of the music and songs. It is worthy of being loved by people, and they will want to watch and listen to it. Opera, whether performed in the time period when the play was created or for the modern age, is a pleasure, an interest in life. The popular plots are often well known to the public; for example, Handel's *Cleopatra*. The plot depicts the ancient civilization of the Egyptian Empire, which was coexisting with the Roman Empire. Cleopatra and Julius Caesar—ruler and dictator of the Roman Empire, Caesar the Great—from their first meeting, fell in love. When Caesar was assassinated, Cleopatra was heartbroken, but she still needed to have the courage to save the world at war. She finally returned to the Mediterranean because of her love for Caesar. The imperial forces maintain a balanced state of equal strength and avoided constant warfare.

I remember that in opera's heyday, some theaters were so crowded that the production had to be divided into several nights. A typical example is Wagner's opera masterpiece *The Ring of Nibelungen*, which can be divided into four parts: "Gold of the Rhine," "Women of the Vulgar," "Siegfried," and "The Twilight of the Gods." It was staged on four nights. In the current environment, perhaps it is economically feasible to perform this drama, but it may be difficult to keep pace with the original era. So even though it is still possible to see the new productions, the music seems much like narrative information, such as in an encyclopedia. The era in which there was a magical depiction of the great opera music may be difficult for modern fans to understand. I think that any long operatic works have the same issue.

Therefore, according to the tradition of this work—playing over a few nights—I also segmented some operas that I judged worthy but too long, like some composers' works, emphasizing independent plays between each final curtain. The final curtains are subtle, intertwined but independent. This has increased my interest in listening and appreciating the opera, especially in the background of the scenes. The material is innocent, but the heroine still longs for the theme of the opera—love. It is suitable for some female characters and some sopranos. This is entirely a personal preference.

As for CD recordings of the opera, it is also a great advantage for opera fans to divide the opera when it has more than twenty or thirty songs. Of course, I still recommend listening to the entire opera while listening. Unlike film viewing, which it is not easy to divide because of the image and visual continuity, the practice of dividing CD recordings is like listening to a taste of opera.

My love of opera and the habit of listening to it started from my listening to the entire CD recordings of the opera. From those recordings—conductor, singers, orchestra, and vintage—I can get a lot of knowledge that inspires and benefits my appreciation. Listening to the opera recordings is fascinating and the sounds of the great singers linger.

Chapter 6

Since the last work of the studio was the "My Opera Experience" anthology, I also reviewed the book while I was busy with my work and during my leisure time.

Some pieces are below:

Article 1—"Opera Tradition and Tenor"

The opera has always had a protagonist who is a baritone, contralto, or a soprano. With the rise of the romantic opera, the male lead tenor in the drama would fall in love with the heroine soprano, who did not resist it completely, and they sang of their love together. The drama is like composer Umberto Giordano's work, *Andrea Chenier*, in which the male and female protagonists sing a duet, calmly and righteously, and finally go to die together. And it is also like Puccini's *Manon Lescaut*. The second scene of the second act has the "duet of love" by the male and female protagonists, with romantic love and passionate sighs.

Thus, the role and position of the tenor in the opera also changed from the lyrical tenor in the classical period, a "leggero" tenor, to a heroic and dramatic role, changing his tone and sound characteristics from the early development of the opera. In 1700, what kind of evolution should there have been? Does only the sound become thicker and the volume become louder?

At this time, I remembered several opera characters that I had heard, such as Edgardo in *Lucia di Lammermoor*, Alfredo in *La Traviata*, Duke Mantova in *Rigoletto*, and Nemorino in the *L'elisir d'amore*, sung by famous lyric tenors. In addition to lyric tenor's wonderful and clear voice, he also has a high-pitched E—a talented person who is born with a rare talent. In the role interpretations, from a doctor, to a student, to a noble duke, and even a farmer, the transformations are like his own characteristics. The characteristics of the voice show a noble temperament and simple features, with rich singing skills. And besides the interpretations of the sound, the successful interpretation of these different roles, even more so, also affected the later singers.

Opera can express mood and satisfy the desire and demand of the spirit.

Recently on Facebook, I saw some master classes of vocal music, but it is always like a flash in the pan—if you do not grasp the opportunity, it will be gone. As a student of vocal music and one who has stood on stage for performances, there is still a long way to the end, and I need to work hard and study an opera aria with the enthusiasm of the stage performer. It is indispensable to achieving great singing. This is hard to come by. Should not we cherish the singers who currently perform on the stage? After all, they have spent a lot of time and energy studying and preparing!

Article 2—"Music Bookstore"

One day I passed through an old district in the city center with a long road, and there were ancient arches and archway buildings on both sides. There was a music bookstore on the road, on the second floor of one of those buildings, that sold music books and musical scores.

I climbed the stairs, went into the bookstore, and started looking. I saw some composers' works—for example, Schubert's, Brahms's, and Schumann's collection of art songs—and it evoked my musical dream. I tried to learn to sing lieder, which refers to German songs from the Romantic period. I restrain myself from buying any more, but I have bought Richard Strauss's collection of art songs. I don't know how to control myself. I have to try hard to learn a song, as so many scores are the same.

Speaking of art songs, I recently was swamped with a German art song CD, *Von Ewiger Liebe*. It is performed by the soprano Anja Harteros and includes composers such as Beethoven, Schubert, Schumann, Richard Strauss, Brahms.

The poetic lyrics of the art songs, the unique rhymes of the unique Germans, the composing style of the above-mentioned composers, and the German style of romance, leisure, calm and quiet, once was my pastime in the evening. And before going to sleep, I liked to listen to an album, sometimes searching through Apple Music and adding it to my favorite collection, and then I'd fall asleep.

The soprano Anja Harteros sings with her simple tone interpretation, without vanity and excessively gorgeous, consistently interpreting these art songs with her spirit in the entire album. If there were a solo vocalist, there would also be a great feast for vocal and artistic songs.

The content of the album, the title of each song, is like a poem. These songs are:

1. Gebet zu Gott
2. An Die Hoffnung
3. Ich Liebe Dich
4. Am See
5. Schwanengesang
6. Gretchen am Spinnrade
7. Wehmut
8. Seligkeit
9. Lied der Suleika
10. Was will die einsame Trane
11. Jemand
12. Venetianische Lieder Nr. 1
13. Venetianische Lieder Nr.2
14. Die Nacht
15. Meinem Kinde
16. Befreit
17. Allerseelen

18. Dein Blaues Ange
19. Liebestreu
20. Wenn du nur Zuweilen lachelst
21. Der Tod, das ist Die kuhle Nacht
22. An ein Veilchen
23. Von ewiger Liebe

Some lyrics have a beautiful artistic component. This is the reason why German art songs have lasted for a long time. To imagine the long-term immersion into the world of love and hate in the opera world, you should you listen to German art songs and lieder. Isn't it a kind of liberation and spiritual sublimation? This metaphysical poetic mood is a type of a cleansing of the mind for the office workers who are busy in their daily lives.

Since listening to opera music often is a long process, in order to develop the habit and taste of listening, I started to record them, including the music that I listen to every day, with certain tracks, composers, and singers.

Chapter 7

ear noon, I went to a nearby bookstore and saw a travel book about Spain. A recent news report mentioned a district in Spain, Catalonia, and the independent referendum there. The Spanish authorities and the Catalonians will hold an independent referendum in two weeks.

The travel book introduces Spain. The country has four dialects. Among them, the language of the central Castile region is the official language. There also are the Galician autonomous region in the north that speaks Galician, the Basque autonomous region that speaks Euskara, and Catalonia, which speaks Catalan as the official language of the place.

Spain has long ruled here as part of it. For more than a hundred years, the province in Spain, like the referendum incidents heard here, has had the same political demands, which have become a test for the Spanish authorities.

Spain is located in the southwest of the European continent. Under the agreement with the European Union, what kind of development will happen?

The Spaniards, Spanish culture, and Spanish language are introduced in the travel book, looking at Spain from the viewpoint of a traveler and a passenger, as well as from the viewpoint of Spaniards, looking at their country. How much is different in these two points? What's the difference?

I am reminded of a travel and language book proposal for this studio, *Travel around Roma, and Speak Italian*, which is divided into several themes and introduces local transportation, stations, how to buy tickets, eating in restaurants, local street culture, churches, and monuments. It also includes most of the popular and easy-to-use Italian phrases, showcasing the practical rhythm of the Italian language, which makes me feel that the charm of European culture is incredible.

The book's directory is as follows:

1. Preface—About Italian: Vocabulary Pronunciation and Grammar
2. Preparations—Preparation before Travel
3. Entry
4. Strolling through Rome
5. Meeting the Locals for the First Time—Piacere
6. Sightseeing Facilities—Subway
7. Local Tavern—Wine Cellar Restaurant
8. Dining Etiquette
9. Meeting Friends
10. Boutique
11. Small Market
12. Café
13. Pizza shop—Pizzeria
14. Ice Cream
15. Share with Friends
16. Conclusion

The book also includes some photos of the landscape, streets, monuments, restaurants, and boutiques in Rome, as well as information on how to get to the monuments, museums, and Vatican and other information.

There are also some views on Rome, from the rise and fall of the historical Roman Empire to the modern, historical, and cultural changes. Rome's charm has been constant for thousands of years, leading travelers to pursue their European dreams.

Work Diary—"Learn Italian"

After I started learning Italian, I gradually learned that the incredible language (and even my own mother tongue) should be well examined for the sources of dialects, foreign words, terminology, and professional terms (for example, in all aspects, law, music, art, cooking).

If the language barrier is a hindrance to understanding the truth of a thing, then learning it, digesting it, absorbing it, and applying it will change these frustrations that are not understood or even misunderstood.

In addition, in terms of law, language pays attention to timeliness, correctness, and judgment. In politics, there may be language gap caused by geography. In film, we see regional differences. The characters in a film decide their own destinies because of misunderstanding or understanding. This is a culture of their own lives, decided by language used, cognition, and reaction.

I often speak in my mother tongue and listen to some foreign countries or ethnicities that are close to mine. This helps to understand my surroundings and daily life. Maybe without air, there is no language. So is a vacuum a kind of silence or a kind of death?

Regarding the sense of powerlessness in politics, do you also feel that it is something that needs to be fully motivated to survive? If you have the same feeling about your current life, isn't it necessary for the body to stand up and move? Therefore, some simple daily lives are so lively.

One day, people will eventually find that language is just the way it exists. That sentence in the language comes from the stagnation of life.

In Italy, a street popular term is "Alla vita fa bene." It is like a daily practice, experience, or just a greeting. When will people understand?

Work Diary—"My Daily Living Expenses"

In the morning, I went to a bank and deposited the rent for the studio into my account. Even though I've had such experience, I still have to do it.

I calculated that the cost of daily living is mostly spent on transportation and food expenses. The transportation fee is a bus and a subway ticket. It costs between thirty-two and forty-eight dollars a month. The food cost is about nine dollars a day, about $279 a month, but I often go to convenience stores, buying water, drinks, fruits, snacks, and so on for three to four dollars a day, about $124 a month. By the end of the month, the maximum amount is calculated, as $48 + $279 + $124 = $451. That's nearly five hundred dollars a month.

I have the pressure of paying studio rent, but this is already a very good material life, and I could spend this day working in the studio. Fortunately, there is political stability here, with no war. What if my life were in jeopardy if war broke out?

If you were unfortunate enough to contract a disease, or if you encountered a business downturn or a depression, you would not be able to prevent it beforehand. The consequences would be unimaginable, let alone there being political instability.

Society's system is old, just as people are older and older. How can we not pay more attention to the importance of health?

I am fortunate that I can have such a good life, taking over the work of the studio. It helps me to avoid the trouble of restlessness in life. I have to say it again: "I have to thank God."

Work Diary—"Economic Cycle, Fourth Quarter"

The weather has gradually turned colder, and the economy has entered the fourth quarter of the year (Q4). If in this year, economics have been cultivated well, then the fourth quarter should be the season for preparing for a bumper harvest.

Recent global news has seen that not only Catalonia in Spain but also the Lombard Province in Italy will hold a referendum. The reason may be the tax issues between the central and local regions or perhaps the global political situation and economic climate.

New photos and reports from the streets of Barcelona indicate that four hundred thousand people took to the streets. Many people feel hopeless and may resort to political ideology. Now, the groups on the streets of Barcelona, Spain, are the same as elsewhere.

This group has sported events and finally returned to the mood and voice of the small citizen, as if nothing had happened. My dear Spain—how does she (the territory) feel?

I think of my establishing the studio. I am looking forward to finding someone I can trust. Maybe I haven't yet because I haven't prayed enough or long enough.

Work Diary—"Winter"

Recently I have discovered that my body is too fat; my gut has a greasy feeling. Therefore, when I went to the fruit market and saw many oranges, I bought some.

This season, with the weather beginning to cool down, is the fruit season for oranges. I found oranges, with colors ranging from green to orange, grown in various places and sold in the fruit market. I bought orange-green oranges most often because orange peel is very beautiful and is rich in vitamin C, which can help prevent illness, such as colds.

As the weather suddenly cooled, I became lethargic. I didn't wake up until eleven o'clock in the morning and didn't eat too much at noon. One day when it was cold, I went to the market stall and ate tempura and radish soup.

I still want to go to the hot springs, but by internet searching, I found that the cost of swimming at the public pool at the tourist hotel is nearly twenty dollars. Obviously, the winter is the best season for the hot-springs hotel, instead of the other places where I can stay.

Work Diary—"Belong to My Little Space"

In my studio, I have a small living space that I can design by myself, and the room is about 78 square yards. The special feature of this space is that half of it is a high-standard living room and the other half has a ceiling height of nearly eighteen feet. The space is divided into upper and lower layers. The furniture is not yet ready; it must be designed first. This has become a problem for me. In addition to asking the interior designer to draw the design, I still have to have a sum of money. I asked the decorator for a price, and he said it would cost about $18,850. I also must have some furniture, which I plan to buy at the furniture store, as follows:

1. a two-person antique sofa
2. upright floor lamp
3. wooden dining table with four chairs
4. table chandelier
5. single bed
6. bedside cabinet
7. full-length vanity side
8. one cabinet
9. desk with a computer chair
10. one LCD TV
11. balcony pot rack
12. kitchenware and tableware
13. toiletries

The problem that is giving me a headache is what kind of space design I should do. However, I won't worry about it myself; I will deal with it with the designer. He suggested that the wall in the living room should not be moved to maintain the original pattern design.

Chapter 8

"Opera Works by Realistic Opera Composer Umberto Giordano" from My Opera Experience

Part 1—*Andrea Chenier*

The news of the opera world, which was known in December, should be the opera composed by Umberto Giordano, *Andrea Chenier*, which is currently being performed at La Scala in Milan. This opera, which was recently launched in Europe, is constantly in rehearsal and being performed, from the British Covent Garden, to the Bavarian State Opera, to the current Milan La Scala Opera House.

The opera is the story of the family of the heroine, Maddalena, and the Andrea Chenier during the French Revolution in 1789. Since the time frame is a revolutionary period, the love story of the so-called "Big Age" is different from the text. For example, the story in the narrative form of the novel has increased focus on the background of the era, the revolutionary period, which was adapted from the plot of the novel, and added the opera music to show the children's sentiments in the revolutionary period.

At that time, in the environment of the corrupt society, the people were living in the poverty and were not tolerant of the aristocrats' daily pampering. The masses protested in the streets, so that the relationship between people is not as kind as that of the authorities. The feeling was that how could people abandon humanity while being eager for the aura of humanity? Such contradiction and reality.

After the beginning of the French Revolution in 1789, the story moves to the aristocratic home of the heroine, Maddalena. For the opening music, the servants are busy, everyone is busy, and the atmosphere is one of pleasure. Everything seemed prosperous—a gratifying sight—because today, a group of guests are coming. In the process of preparation, the ladies are so full of dreams and longing because Maddalena's admired knight, Andrea Chenier, is also among the guests. Maddalena is happy, as is everyone, but she does not know her story, her own life. This scene today will be the prelude.

From then on, she and Andrea will become the sole figures in the story. Together, they complete a French love story after the outbreak of the French Revolution. Regrettably, this story does not end with marriage but the tragedy of the male and female protagonists, who go to the execution ground together and lose their heads.

Maddalena was a naive girl, but she also felt the revolutionary smell of her surroundings. How could she be so lucky and have a happy life?

The guests arrived at the mansion. The first scene is a living room salon. The scenes of are the meeting with friends and relatives and feeling the warmth of the people, but soon everyone starts calling for Knight Andrea to make an impromptu poem, accompanied by the piano. He sings, "Un di all'azzuro spazio …" (or "One of them among the blue sky …").

> Un di all'azzuro spazio
> Guardai profondo,
> e ai prati colmi di viole,
> Pioveva loro I'll sole,
> e folgorava d'oro il mondo.

The poem sings his enthusiasm for the motherland, but the background and atmosphere of the Revolution are reminiscent of the knight's—a patriotic poet—dissatisfaction with the political situation and ambition that's full of reform.

Amazingly, Andrea suddenly turns his head and asks Maddalena in one sentence, making Maddalena's eyes more melancholy.

Back in the French Revolution, the environment at the time was full of untrustworthiness. In this case, what could be relied upon for safeguarding Maddalena's life? Life was not guaranteed, so how could Maddalena have any expectations for love?

In the second scene, Andrea appears in a restaurant and in the streets of Paris. He says that his ambition is to travel abroad. His identity as a patriotic poet caught the attention of the authorities. He still longs for Maddalena, and they part with grief. Later, he meets a lady from Maddalena's family and sends a message to Maddalena. Andrea is about to travel abroad. Unexpectedly, Maddalena suspected this and went to meet him. She came to see Andrea when it was nearly midnight. Like a dreamy encounter, Andrea and Maddalena sing a duet of love and parting. Maddalena finally unburdens her heart and confesses her love to Andrea. The mood of the duet was like a dream. The long-awaited couple cling to each other and sing in unison, "Together!"

The third act shows that Andrea was arrested by the authorities because of the tension. Maddalena goes to the court's secretary, Gerard, to plead for his release. She has courage, different from her shyness in the first act. She sings the famous aria of the play, "La mamma morta." This aria shows a change in her life. After this, her character moves in one direction, and that is death. As far as Maddalena is concerned, perhaps death is only for her mother's body, which has disappeared from Maddalena's life, but Maddalena's mother's love is constant. Maddalena chooses to impersonate and replace a female death-row inmate. She goes to the execution ground and dies. At the moment of Maddalena's death, did she finally get together with her mother?

In the fourth act, Andrea finally collapses in his cell. The second aria, "Come un bel di maggio," is like a beautiful day in May. Maddalena is coming soon. Paying jailers at the prison, the two meet, each time with mixed feelings, and they sing a duet of touching love, with mutual feelings in their hearts. The two encourage and support each other and sing together the final long song as they approach the execution, the end of the play.

The play *Andrea Chenier* is a realist opera, but the music contains quite a lot of lyric elements. The love story of the two people in the drama, in the context of this revolutionary period, can especially resonate with the viewers, especially when the male and female protagonists go to the execution ground and choose to go to the death together. It seems to prove that their love for each other transcends the revolutionary environment and overcomes and transcends the Revolution. At the end of the game, two men sing high praises. How did they inspire the time and space? It not only inspired the young men and women of the revolutionary period but also inspired the audience who watched the drama. It is really a sensation and offers realism across and through time, space, and even opera itself.

I cannot help but wonder, if the subject matter were changed—for example, to be composed by Donizetti or Verdi—how would such realism be presented? Perhaps we can look at *La Favorita* by Donizetti as like Andrea Chenier's story, as well as Verdi's description of human rights and looting in his late composing period, such as *Aida*, through the identity of the Egyptian female slave, who presents a desire for human rights and the yearning for freedom. At the end of the drama, Aida chose to go to Huang Quan with her beloved one, Radames, and the musical symbol has a human sublimation. From the beginning of its prelude, it contains such a spirit.

And final scene of *Andrea Chenier* shows the French national consciousness, the desire for freedom, and the rise of human-rights awareness. It is a symbol and commemoration of the people who experienced the Revolution.

Part 2—*Fedora*

Talking about the opera work of Umberto Giordano, there is another famous one, *Fedora*, which tells the story of the Princess Fedora, who, behind the scenes, is trying to help rescue the gentleman, Loris Ipanoff. *Fedora* has a similar plot to the play *Andrea Chenier*. It doesn't point out the good and the bad, or the right and wrong. It is interpreted and played by the opera actors. Among them, the progress of the plot is completely in accordance with logic, and perhaps the plot has a clue, but it does not drag in the water, and it is likely a thought-provoking drama.

In the first act, Fedora returns to the villa from the outside. After seeing the flowers in the room, she could not help but recall her dead husband and the past. From outside, military police, doctors, and a seriously injured man enter the room. Fedora also found it strange when documents were stolen, and the people speculated about the main suspect of these incidents. Then a small servant recalled, "Ipanoff!" The crowd was horrified. The doctor came out and declared that the seriously wounded man had been paralyzed. Fedora prayed for the dead.

In the second act, the opening is a waltz-style. Fedora is at the villa banquet. Ipanoff is on the scene, introduced by friends, and Fedora knows and then sings the famous short song, "Amor ti vieta." After that, the guests go to the piano together, with the piano master playing Chopin's work. That leaves two people, Fedora and Ipanoff. Fedora is eager to prove Ipanoff's innocence at the moment, but Ipanoff is concerned about her, and the two decide that after the meeting, they will talk about it. Then Ipanoff exits.

Fedora, at this time, decides to rescue Ipanoff. The background music of Chopin has just ended, and it is immediately replaced by a brisk dance, but the czar's bad news comes by way of a servant, and the party ends. Fedora is alone, and her theme music begins. As the music plays, she writes a letter and confesses to the aftermath. After that, the waiter informs her that Ipanoff has arrived and the two meet.

Ipanoff tells her his story. His mother, brother, and sister-in-law were confused and helpless, and they still have no solution in reality. The two people finally sing, "T'amo!" ("I love you!"), which ends the second act.

Act III begins in a mountain forest garden. Fedora and Ipanoff and customers are there. They are on vacation together. However, one of customers advises Fedora on how to solve Ipanoff's lawsuit. While Fedora hesitates, a messenger brings a letter. Ipanoff reads that after knowing his mother's current situation, he went on and saw that his brother was reinstated. Even though Fedora was persuaded, he still lost his mind to his long-repressed family. Fedora takes a poison pill that was hidden in the cross she wears on her chest. The folk songs of children's voices come from afar. It seems that this unfortunate story is also heard.

Like the play *Andrea Chenier*, such as Maddalena's encounter, her fate from her birth, and her courage for love, such was Fedora's attempt to rescue Ipanoff (and Maddalena's to rescue Andrea). Both show touching and noble sentiments—although in the moment, people may not understand this noble sentiment. In this context, Andrea Chenier appeared in Maddalena's aria, "La mamma morta," while Fedora appeared, singing her love theme, which is like the Chinese concept: "You say it best when you say nothing at all."

However, to satisfy the psychological needs of the audience and the educational significance of the opera, those two are like the two ends of a balance. How to make a choice among the playwright, the composer, and the director during the performance depends on how well could they create the play.

Chapter 9

Work Diary—Proposal of the Studio about
My New Year's Life Proposal

The book *My New Year's Life Proposal* is inspired by *My Happy Life Proposal* by Miss Gretchen Rubin, who takes action and the theme of love's home from the point of view of a housewife. As a starting point, she changes her family's lifestyle, starting with herself. Not only did she change herself, but her husband, children, and in-laws were also affected by her plans, and their lives were improved. Setting daily life goals is one of the examples of the author's project with "happy by growth." Starting with her, it then affects more people, and she tells her family and friends about her plans, inviting them to participate in her project, and so they live happier, more fulfilling lives and grow more.

And for *My New Year's Life Proposal*, I not only try to plan a New Year's new project but also look back at what happened in the previous year for the plan I have done or the unfulfilled or unfinished part of the review.

The contents of the plan are as follows,

1. Begin a habit of exercise and fitness.
2. Change my eating habits.
3. Drink only alcohol-free drinks.
4. Stop eating sweets and snacks.
5. Meet with the studio members once a month.

6. Travel abroad—make a business trip plan.
7. Find several ways to cool off from the heat.
8. Go to the beach.
9. Research my fund investment.
10. Go hiking.
11. Do online shopping.
12. Prepare for Christmas and New Year's.

Work Diary—"After Two Months"

Since the beginning of December, I have moved into a new house and started a new job in the studio. I set a timetable for myself. In the morning after breakfast, I will review the meaning of the language. In the afternoon, I will do some routine work in the studio to see the files and records. I will make calls and see if there are any new messages on the answering machine.

Recently, the focus of the studio has been the novel called *Summer Dreams*. According to the publisher, the results from the trial reading are very good. Even some filmmakers have heard about it and are interested in the subject matter of this novel. There are plans to buy the rights to it and then adapt it to a screenplay. Such a range of influence may spread throughout all English-speaking countries, regions, and cities, so I have to be careful.

At the end of the workday, I came back to my new home, thinking about visiting a furniture store, purchasing some home decorations, sending away the old furniture, and completing my new living room.

After these two months, I also have some new ideas. I also want to write a few proposals, and I hope the sponsor (boss) can accept them.

I want to have a companion who is eager to have a new home.

After returning from the trip to Italy, I have also raised the idea of going once again. I always make a trip myself because I don't have a travel companion. I think, though, that traveling on my own can be restricting when it comes to seeing the city attractions and arranging the journey. For one person to get there, there are so many things to achieve.

On the first night after I arrived in Rome, I listened to the sounds outside the window all night. The pedestrians on the street chatted all night, and I almost didn't fall asleep. The next morning, many military police were on the streets of Rome, patrolling the road around the train station.

A person's travel has unexpected joy and can be a lot of fun, but the situation on the streets of Rome caused me to be alert. I shouldn't live alone or even plan to live alone for a lifetime.

After several months, many things have happened—some have solutions; some have no solution. But time is still passing, and the world is still turning. Fortunately, sometimes I hear news. Some people are still working hard in this world, and I have to appreciate their fearless courage.

Now, I only have a freelance class once a week, and I am in contact with my colleagues in the studio and in the publishing house.

At the same time, I am also writing about my favorite opera music—some writing after watching the opera—especially about the female characters in the opera, the female vocalists. I sometimes have an amazing idea—*le idee*. I feel that they come to me and talk to me, like whole daisies, whole flowers. Sometimes, the amount is too much for me to bear, as if it's telling me that this piece is one side of my real life, and sometimes I have to be careful. It overlaps with my real life, perhaps because after I wrote some papers, I decided to start writing a novel—the story—and attempt to make it concrete.

This means that I decided to no longer let the words float in the air, empty, with no record. As in filming using cameras, or painters using images, novelists record in words, capturing the beauty, aesthetics, beauty of that moment and even the indescribable expression of feelings.

I will follow the example of some great masters and great men, and I will never give up.

Chapter 10

*I*n the year 2017, I started work on the Opera Music and Education Foundation. In late May 2017, I started to record my opera video using the Apple Music app. Concerts and other music materials are available on You Tube. Let me do a year of review.

In May, I was immersed in the baroque vocal operas, such as Handel's *Alcina*. Fortunately, on YouTube, there was a full-length version starring by Patricia Petibon and Philippe Jaroussky. After watching, I wrote the following: *Since watching Handel's opera Alcina, I began to think that I could be like the protagonist, Ruggiero, and that Alcina would enter my new home and my life on that beautiful day.*

In addition to this play, I also listened to at least two different versions of *Manon* bye Massenet, and I made a version for comparison, including the following:

1. a recording of the collaboration of Mirella Freni and Luciano Pavarotti
2. a recorded version of Victoria de los Angeles and Henri Legay
3. a video version of Mirella Freni's performance in her hometown, Modena

All of the above are quite precious music materials.

Next, I watched a few of Signora Mirella Freni's performances, including Fedora by Umberto Giordano. I watched the following versions:

1. with partner Placido Domingo in the Metropolitan Opera House, New York
2. with Placido Domingo and La Scala in Milan, Italy
3. with Jose Carreras in Rome
4. with Sergio Larin in the Politeama Theater in Palermo, Italy, in 1998

Later, another *Fedora* version appeared on YouTube, but it could only be classified as music material. It was nearly thirty years ago, and it was the version of the protagonist, Signora Daniella Dessi.

In the month of June, Italians celebrated the National Day of Italy on June 2, and I listened to *I Puritani* on YouTube. The protagonists were portrayed by Luciano Pavarotti and Mirella Freni, with the cooperation of the famous conductor, Maestro Riccardo Muti, in 1971. Another version was from 1969, in which Alfredo Kraus sang his version of Arturo, and Mirella Freni was deeply impressive singing the Atto I finale's high-C long treble. It was a live recording, and the audience's reaction and applause were warm.

In addition, in late June 2017, in Covent Garden, London, Verdi's *Otello* was performed. On July 10, I wrote an article about this opera. The actor was Wagner tenor Jonas Kaufmann, and it's contained in the collection of "My Opera Experience I."

At the same time, in Bologna, there was a performance of Donizetti's *Lucia di Lammermoor,* and on that day, I woke up early in the morning to listen to the Atto III finale on the Italian radio Rai 3. The reaction was again overwhelming.

During summer vacation, July and August, I was fascinated by the vocalist Anja Harteros's German art album, *Von Ewiger Liebe,* which included Beethoven, Schumann, Schubert, Richard Strauss, and Brahms's lieder.

In addition, Dame Kiri Te Kanawa's personal online radio platform also offers many of her personal signature songs, as well as the ethnic music of her native New Zealand Maori, who have spent a lot of time with me! There is also a CD album called *Kiri* that I've added to my favorites.

In order to study the bel canto, I listened to the recordings of the current popular opera singers, such as Angela Gheorghiu and Natalie Dessay. Especially mentioned here is Angela Gheorghiu, who rose to prominence in the Royal Opera House in the opera *La Traviata* in 1994. In February 2018, she was also busy with Puccini's *Tosca*, performing with Erwin Schrott, as Scarpia, at the Vienna State Opera House. Her acting career has spanned more than twenty years, and her name has been included in music dictionaries. She is a rare lyrical drama soprano. Her voice in the middle and low range has a gentle, feminine beauty; the sound is beautiful, and the treble is bright and free with penetration. In October 2017, the new album was launched—Angela Gheorghiu's *Eternamente—The Verismo Album*. The scope of her performance has entered the field of realist opera.

In addition, professional opera singers who also released solo albums in 2017 include Jonas Kaufmann (*L'Opera*) and Joseph Calleja (*Verdi*).

In addition, Patricia Petibon also has many well-received solo albums. She specializes in baroque bel canto singing, especially her *French Baroque Arias* album, which has also joined my favorite-CDs list.

Lucia di Lammermoor is still my favorite opera, especially the Lucia as interpreted by the opera goddess diva Maria Callas. It can be called the quintessential Lucia, and her reputation is legendary. And another new edition of *Lucia* is from new-generation actor Piotr Beczala as Edgardo and the actress Natalie Dessay as Lucia. This should be the latest *Lucia* version. The tenor Piotr Beczala also is famous for playing the role of Faust in *Faust*, which is also his famous opera character. It is unforgettable. Not long ago in the Vienna State Opera's production of Verdi's *Un Ballo in Maschera*, the character of Riccardo leads the show—YouTube has a full-length opera performance. The characters of Amelia and Oscar, and the baritone protagonist, Renato, are all portrayed by actors who sing very well. It is the best cast in recent memory.

In early December 2017, *Andrea Chenier* was performed at La Scala by the soprano Anna Netrebko, and with Yusif Eyvazov as the male protagonist, which was a grand event in the opera world at the end of that year. Fans of operatic art all wanted to go to Milan to gather as a pilgrimage.

In late December, Puccini's *La Boheme* was performed at the

Berlin City Opera House in Berlin, starring Piotr Beczala and Angela Gheorghiu, with a Christmas atmosphere to celebrate the end of 2017.

In addition, the Christmas music album I collected from Apple Music—*Christmas with Kiri Te Kanawa—Live at the Royal Opera House*—also accompanied me through the Christmas season.

These are the musical opera performances that I collected from May to December 2017. They will also be recorded in the database of the Opera Music and Education Foundation.

I think that time has entered into the postmodern era. People have already undergone major revolutions and changes in their feelings, tastes, and preferences for listening. Opera is a popular product of the seventeenth and eighteenth centuries. The gap, then, is nearly three hundred years. Many people yearn for that era, and I am one of them. The stage of "yearning for the ancients" is starting, much like people long for their loved ones—parents, grandparents. And so this homesickness is like their love of opera.

Chapter 11

*R*ecently, the new opera season in Europe began. In April 2018, in Italy, there was a production of *Simon Boccanegra*, the work of the opera master Giuseppe Verdi. At the Metropolitan Opera House in New York, there were performances of *Turandot* by Puccini and another opera, *Luisa Miller*, in which the tenor Piotr Beczala collaborated with Placido Domingo. April 11 was the date of the premiere of *Lucia di Lammermoor*, starring another tenor Vittorio Grigolo. Four plays at once—this is a busy opera world. In particular, the Metropolitan Opera House, New York, has taken up three of them, and I don't know if such a busy performance schedule will make the stage production and scenery too busy.

I am also beginning to suspect that the promotion of the "beautiful singing"—bel canto—has been revived than the performances, which continually unearths younger opera singers with and more potential.

Although I live with music and appreciate the writing of essays and narratives, there are still many things in my daily life waiting for me to gradually understand and complete.

Originally, I planned to buy an iPad mini for processing text, paperwork, editing, and so on. As a result, one day when I was browsing the internet, I found a new product, a mobile screen amplifier. I think of the proposal. The studio is equipped with an iPhone as the company cellular phone for contacting various entities, such as the boss, colleagues, the publishing house, and so on. With this screen amplifier, I can directly use the phone, but it has the effect of an iPad. The amplifier can be enlarged to a maximum of twelve inches and may even replace the iPad Pro that I originally planned to purchase. The price is $1,090. Thanks to modern technology, everything is really convenient.

So I continued to browse the web and saw a wireless Bluetooth headset, which is a mobile power device. The headset can be recharged by putting it back in the box.

I think of the accounts that our studio has on Facebook and YouTube. There are many opera-related clips, short videos, full-screen opera videos, celebrity interviews, and so on. If this screen amplifier is connected to the wireless Bluetooth headset by this iPhone, I can become a small audio-visual studio.

I received an email from New York, asking for advice on the cover of the book *Summer Dreams*, which they edited and published.

I used the photo-selection software to view a lot of photos on the theme of summer and then used the poster-design software to do the subsequent design processing.

I saw some photos of landscapes, food, tableware, and upholstery. Finally, I selected a photo with summer sun and a tea set on the tea table. The content of the photo gives me a leisurely and cozy feeling, which is in line with the sentiment of this novel. It's a story that describes an office worker who become part of the SoHo community, and the topic of the story is popular with the background environment at that time. The influence of LOHAS (Lifestyle of Health and Sustainability) has changed his lifestyle, life pace, and attitude toward life. Finally, he finds the meaning of life.

I used the poster and photo-editing software to paste the photo, and I chose to edit the font, font size, and the title of the book, *Summer Dreams*, along with the author's pen name.

Then I replied to a coordinator in New York, sending an email with file of the designed poster cover.

The studio works on the other side regarding this part of the Opera Music and Education Foundation. I reviewed some of the ideas of the former studio director, such as the title of the foundation, the chairman, the address of manager, and the phone number. There are five member places for sponsors or companies and organizations. There is a previous contact number on the top; some of them have been tested, and some are empty.

One of the people who answered the phone seemed to be the relative of the previous director in charge. I saw that there were some records of conversations on the manuscript, similar to the minutes of a meeting, which were nothing more than comments on the operation of the foundation.

The content also mentioned an opera that was staged in London at the time. This is obviously the theme he set. The purpose might have been to write a special article to report on advertising and to promote the upcoming opera in London.

The content of some sentences caught my attention.

"The play code of the old production and rehearsal has a certain reputation," and "Quite fierce competition."

It was also noted that it was "performed in winter."

Other interesting comments included the following:

- "How can I afford it?"
- "Temperature, humidity, climate during the period."
- "The interest of the audience."
- "The two dramas are the same as the story of the love triangle."
- "Love the enemy."
- "Or a coercion."
- "How do actors perform murder on the bright stage?"
- "There is a duet of love in the play."
- "If such a plan is put on hold because I am not active, I will feel sorry for myself!"
- "At present, the assistance and manpower I can get is very limited. They are all free-spirited liberals. We all have ideals, and we are often trapped in it, and we are unable to extricate ourselves. The hands help each other; no one is truly wholehearted, and no one really wants to be."

Suddenly, the doorbell of the studio rang. I went to answer the door. It turned out to be a courier. He brought a box of crepe cakes. I looked at the sender's name, and the name was familiar.

After a graduate came to the interview and talked with the boss (one of the sponsors), the boss asked me if I had just graduated, would I recommend him?

> My first recommendation was that he should come to work in the company.
> Second recommendation: he should run for public office.
> Third recommendation: get married.

As a result of our discussion, it was most beneficial for him to get married first. In the current situation, it was difficult for him to concentrate on work when life was uncertain. However, a stable relationship could change this situation. Therefore, a more appropriate approach was to get married first. In a marital relationship, two people support each other's life and sense of responsibility, and their unclear parts gradually become contoured with each other.

For two people in a relationship, if they have maintained the relationship, two people may be more secure than one. If one side can make a request and the other can accept that, then the combined life can have a new opportunity.

However, what if the party who first proposed the marriage changes his or her mind? Why, in the current era, are both men and women are so reluctant to make a promise?

I looked down at the box of crepe cakes, opened it, went to the counter, took out a cup and tea bag, and made a cup of tea for myself.

I turned on the TV, turned the channel at random, and suddenly went to the movie channel. Sometimes, in the afternoon, this station aired a brilliant movie with a good review.

The plot of the film revolved around a female writer. She looked like a teenager; at least she looked like a young woman. Then, she started to write novels, and the first novel was published and was a success. Later, in order to find a new writing theme, she wrote about a younger girl. The young girl seemed to be smaller than the heroine, and she dared to play at love with men. The female writer used her story as a writing theme in her new novel. Unexpectedly, she developed writer's block. Her issue was the same as the heroine in the story she wrote. She also began to take drugs and drink alcohol, and she developed emotional problems. The female writer also continued her writing.

However, before this, she knew that if she stepped on the brakes, she would not continue her novel. If she could detoxify, abstain from alcohol, or choose to break up with her boyfriend or friends, would the story not develop anymore?

However, at this time in her novel, the plot had made new progress and had reached the end. In the story, the boy came back to ask the girl for forgiveness, treated the girl well, and was willing to rebuild their old relationship, and she agreed. The typing speed of female writers is brisk, and everything eventually ended well.

The processing method of the film made the heroine in the story become mysterious and unpredictable. I began to feel confused. Was the young woman the author of the book, the heroine in the story, or the story of the novel in the drama.

I turned off the TV and continued my afternoon tea, the sun shone in from the window, and the shadows cast by the furniture in the room moved, little by little.

Today, a very beautiful melody lingers in my mind. Now that I think of it, this melody is in the second act of the opera *Andrea Chenier*, the duet of love and leaving of the male and female protagonists in Paris, under a sewer, near midnight—the long-awaited private meeting.

I went out at noon, walked down the street, and went to lunch. The melody still accompanied me along the way, following me across the street, into the restaurant; following me for lunch; following me back and into the studio again.

I suddenly realized that this was the theme of love, the song to which two people fall in love. I live in the world of the love of two people during the day, and they fall in love, and their love accompanies me.

They live in an era of no revolution, only a private life with revolutionary backgrounds.

I think of the box of crepe cakes delivered earlier, thinking about the postmodern-age commitment of people to the future. In this context, the opera story is so prominent and touching, which makes me emotional.

Chapter 12

One modern topic I've considered is "Silent Coffee Shop." I walked down the streets of the city, looking at the beauty of the city all the way, passing by several cafés, which were stylishly quaint, and some were full of customers.

I also observed the guests sitting in the cafés at this time. Some sat in the high chairs by the windows, and some sat at the square tables of two or four people. Three or four people were sitting on a sofa around a low table, and some others were single guests. Some people were chatting; others worked on a notebook computer, seeming serious and focused.

I think that young men and women are so happy in this modern era. I am looking forward to it. I did wonder—if I were twenty years younger and had grown up in a postmodern environment, how happy would it be?

In the coffee shop, customers sat in groups with their own friends. They could communicate and share with each other, and go out to play together. For example, they might go to a concert of a singer or travel together, having a partner for their activities. They might not have to work like some office workers—to go to work every day or get up early to participate in the morning report meeting.

I speculated that most of them were self-employed—they were their own bosses, they opened their own stores, and they hired employees for the store, which gave them time to have leisure time and leisure activities. In the afternoon, they come to the coffee shop for a cup of coffee, use a laptop, remotely control their stores or reports, and feel that the image created is very fashionable for the quality of work and quality of life.

They are dressed in a stylish, minimalist style, and the entire person exudes elegance.

My work and work environment has always been fast and efficient, until I found the work of the studio. I am used to working in awkward and fast environments, and as a result, I developed some occupational diseases.

In the presence of my boss, the image and elegance of our self-distribution became my homework and focus, which I had to learn after I took over the work of the studio.

I think the people in the cafés also browsed online blogs. Some bloggers, or moderators, shared their experiences. I thought, *Some articles and work might be done in these cafés while drinking a cup of coffee.* The attitude of maturity, self-confidence, and independence that was evident out throughout was fascinating.

Perhaps the blog's article sharing was also their sideline job, helping them earn some extra money.

Time is money.

There are also some well-known figures in the industry, some are popular and are read on the postmodern network. The videos they play on the network platform becomes the postmodern replacement TV— the boring and lonely pastime.

Some of them have also participated in singing competitions on TV programs. Their singing skills don't rival some popular pop stars.

What can singing do? They can be placed on their own platforms. Through the distribution and playback of online media, their songs can be shared with many listeners, viewers, and explorers. Many people listen to share, reprint, or set up a fan group. This is the way in which postmodern young people become famous, and everything depends on their own operation of the web platform.

"Net red" can also be classified as a postmodern occupation. Or trading in commodities can also be transformed into a store. What a fulfilling life! Could there be a more desirable working mode?

This also falsifies the negative impression of the internet, which a lot of motivated young people use for their work. Finally, they launch their own brands over time.

Just this month, I bought online four times. I bought clothes, books, and CDs.

Those who go shopping on the street still can't buy the goods they want. It is a very practical and very convenient way to shop by browsing the internet and searching for the products that they really need and want to buy.

It's no wonder that coffee shops sometimes have so many single guests, all focused and silent, using their own laptops or iPads.

Coffee, by itself, also represents the fashionable taste.

I am imagining that one day, I will find a coffee shop somewhere in the city, but this is a silent coffee shop. In this shop, you don't need to talk; you can naturally do what you like. You can slowly enjoy the taste of a cup of coffee. How does it work for the body? Its coffee beans are ground into powder; then there is its charcoal flavor, its sugar, its creamer or milk, and its other spice additives. Next, don't even think about anything else.

A cup of coffee and a leisurely time will have a different taste when everything is not needed. So from here, do you get different feelings?

No need to wait. Chat with friends in advance, and you can have a good time in the afternoon.

Chapter 13

*A*lthough the novel *Summer Dreams* had been handed over to American publishers, I had to do some retrospectives in order to make this English version of the novel perfect.

There is a certain part of the story in this novel, and I will start from there. I think this is also a place where readers will be more easily impressed. I turned on the computer and found the file, which contained many tourist photos.

There were some places of interest in the sightseeing sites. It seemed that the original author was very lucky. The weather was good. It was a sunny day. There were some clouds in the sky, but the sky was blue, and the sunshine was beautiful.

There also was food available for lunch—salads, steamed rice with mushrooms, and white wine. The shape of the glass was beautiful. It seemed to be an antique restaurant. Inside the restaurant it was very dark. There were antique mirrors with gold cornices on the wall, and there were roundabout corridors. It seemed full of friends. I noticed that not only the wine glass but even the food was placed on the antique plate, which was gold rimmed. The note on the photo indicated this was a fine dining restaurant with three Michelin stars.

Later, the author also took a photo of another person at the entrance; standing next to him was a young woman with a very fair skin. This Michelin-starred high-class antique restaurant had a mysterious and elegant charm and atmosphere.

I guessed maybe this was a "semi–self–help" trip, because, in a short while, I saw another photo of another restaurant. This was an open-air restaurant. I guess the author was having afternoon tea because the meal was a delicate sliced-fruit platter that contained strawberries, oranges, kiwis, pineapples, and grapes, with a bottle of sparkling mineral water and a half bottle of lemon black tea. Guests at other tables were also photographed. One of them was a white-haired old man, but his body was very heathy-looking, and he had reddish-brown skin. He was sitting on a chair at the high table and was looking at his phone.

Next in this file were some street scenes. According to the plot of the original novel, I speculated that the background was Europe, perhaps evident from the Italians mentioned in the story. There were some old house numbers and streets with mature trees. I saw a familiar scene, "Spanish Scalinata." Sure enough, there was a boat-break fountain, but the fountain looked very new. Obviously, this historic fountain had been refurbished. The bottom of the fountain reservoir revealed light green water that looked quite cool and comfortable. The shape of the ship also was very special, like a whaling ship. A spring was inside to feed the fountain, and the outer two parts were both classical and modern.

Next was a photo of the windows of some boutiques. There also were many pedestrians on the street. It seemed clean, stylish, and confident. It was really worthy of Rome. There also were many small dresses or evening dresses in the window of the boutiques, which looked fashionable and practical and quite suitable for some occasions.

I saw some pictures the author had taken after returning to the hotel, photos of the spoils and goods. I guess there were net products—some short socks, medium socks, and a pair of sailing shoes that looked very soft and comfortable. The color was black or dark purple.

Then, I couldn't help but laugh; there was the most fashionable underwear and close-fitting clothes. The colors were white, light gray, and flesh-colored. They were packed in a flat, small cardboard box with fashionable models on the top of the box. I saw its asking price—one for sixty-five dollars, which was really expensive, but the underwear seemed comfortable and stylish.

There might also be small souvenirs to bring back to give people, such as a small calendar with antique paintings, although it was five years old, and some metal keyrings. It is also possible to see the crafts of Italy. The color of the metal was very beautiful and very simple. The shape was ordinary, but there was a special feeling. The printed calendar felt special too, as it showed a young woman holding a baby. And the color was a combination of orange, pink, and yellow, often used in antique paintings. The entire atmosphere was soft and indescribably peaceful.

I saw a Roma Pass, a map of Rome that is sold in train stations or in some small stalls and newsstands, a Roman subway ticket, another map, and an open date, detailing the Rome Museum and opening-time instructions. Passengers with a Roma Pass have preferential treatment or discounts to visit museums.

Next it was lunchtime. Maybe the author was vegetarian because the photo seemed to be a plate of salad, and it was a large plate with sliced tomatoes, melons, and perilla, with some sea-salt blocks. Below there was lettuce, and I guessed it was a bottle of olive oil and a small bottle of beer. It seemed to be a great sunny afternoon.

I speculated that perhaps drinking water in Italy was expensive, so a kind of steam water called Frizzante, or other drinks, such as beer, were the most common drink. Because the prices were similar, most tourists would choose drinks instead of drinking water.

There also was a dessert after the meal, a famous dessert in Italy called tiramisu, as well as vanilla ice cream. This seemed to be in the plot of the *Summer Dreams* story.

The two argued over whether to get the tiramisu or the vanilla ice cream. Finally, they broke up, and no one knew that after they left each other, they secretly went back for dessert. In other dessert shops, one person ordered these two desserts.

The charm of Italy really was not only in this one.

There were quite a lot of photos, with the author's big shots. Maybe those I'd seen were just a three-day highlight of his journey.

I continue to pull out the English version of *Summer Dreams*. I wanted to see the plot after he returned to his hometown. The two protagonists have communicated because of their misunderstanding. Has their relationship improved? Do they find a solution? After all, they have been in contact for almost a year.

I suddenly saw a comment in the book: "I don't want this."

It was a small sinker; maybe he bought it to please her.

I can't help but want to ask the heroine, "What do you want in the end?"

However, the actor of this novel did not speak; he returned to his place of residence and stayed up all night.

In the next scene, the actor accepts the hospital's scheduled examination and is ready to have an MRI (magnetic resonance image) taken.

The excerpts below are from a fragment of *Summer Dreams*:

> "There are many things, many of which I don't want to touch again."
> "What do you think is the definition of happiness for two people?"
> "Traveling abroad and immigration are two things."
> "You will never return to youth."
> "My perception is different from what it was in my youth."
> "A chance to start a fight."
> "I have no fate like this."
> "How long will it take for the summer to come again?"
> "I slowly and again found the joy of getting along with me."
> "She said her parents and her family are problems."
> "Why do you cry when you hear his experience?"
> "But while I am thinking of you, I will be sad."
> "Maybe this is a test and training given to me by God."
> "Interpersonal alienation has become a feature of the modern metropolis. Some people still misunderstand it as a fashion."
> "I value my family, but I also long for the comfort of my friends."
> "What is loneliness?"
> A silence.

For the time being, I don't know what I can do.

I am reminded of an email I received this morning. Its content suggested how and when to end the book.

When is it time to end a story?

The next day, I continued the review of *Summer Dreams*. I saw a missed call on the answering machine. It had come in later than eight o'clock last night; it was now afternoon. The US time was midnight. I thought there was no need to return the call immediately.

I opened the archive of the novel. When the story came up on the screen, the hero still was in the country and had not met the heroine yet; he lived alone. There was a trail that he had to walk every morning, whether sunny or rainy. He got up in the morning. After grooming himself, he went to the nearby cafe. His mood was different every day. Sometimes he walked with a smile, sometimes with a melancholy look, sometimes with no expression, and sometimes he looked pale.

He came to the breakfast shop, which sold coffee. He ate sandwiches and a kind of black tea that contained a mixture of flowers and tea. The color of black tea was beautiful; it was a deep red. Sometimes he also ate sandwiches of different flavors, or a toast with a pesto cream butter. At this time, if he wanted to drink coffee, there was only one kind of caramel-milk coffee in the breakfast shop. He then ate toast and drank coffee. After going back home, he felt discomfort in his stomach, similar to gastrointestinal ulcers, but it happened near noon after eating.

The seats in the store had two rows, arranged at a right angle. He liked the row near the side. There were floor-to-ceiling windows. He could see the shade outside the window, and this side was quieter. He sometimes came in a hurry, and after his meal, his heartbeat slowed down. He didn't even move, didn't think about anything; he just sat quietly.

As the light and shadow of the morning gradually increased, the sun shone on the entire wall. It was almost time for him to get up and go home.

I stopped reading here.

I realized I didn't know about his sleep quality. He seemed to get up early if he went to bed early. Was it so he could have enough spirit to face the activities of the next day?

Why did he sometimes seem to be depressed?

This was like a scene in a movie. Why was life so heavy for him?

Didn't he enjoy the so-called LOHAS lifestyle, of which the average office worker was extremely envious?

Observing him from real life, the result of my own observations was that I found out there were not a few unhappy people. I wondered why they seemed to have a freer lifestyle and living space, which should be envied by the office workers who had to work. Why?

This also was reflected in some less–well-known TV series.

The female protagonist was in tears in the corner. The hero bought flowers and bought jewelry in an attempt to comfort her. Why did the couples look like they were not happy at all? Did they not enjoy the sweetness of love?

Why?

Why on earth? I began to imagine the hero in the story of *Summer Dreams*. After the era of the nobles, he was an aristocrat. He was from a royal family. This kind of plot is much more reasonable because of his aristocratic identity. He was different. Just like in police films and thriller movies, all roles are the police but each has a different status, such as grassroots police officers, undercover police, FBI detectives, and so on.

The hero in *Summer Dreams* might be a poet, like Andrea in the opera *Andrea Chenier*, maybe because he himself is like a poem, or he is "poetry."

I had found the direction. The difference in this story was that the hero was a noble poet, not a knight. If he wrote a poem in the story or revealed a little martial arts in the formal education of the nobility, then it was not only popular with female readers.

The first quarter to one-third of the story described his life alone, and he was so deep and melancholy. Like at the French court, the nobles wore dark-blue velvet coats.

Then I fantasized that his life, his education, his taste, and his temperament exuded an elegance and charm.

So, of the images of the heroine in several classic romantic movies, which one is suitable for him? Vivien Leigh, Audrey Hepburn, or Julie Andrews?

This novel—is it just a love story in a popular movie?

I remembered the plot he mentioned. After he first met the heroine, he became happy. His life was full of love, and he became lovely and happy after he fell in love. His life changed, and he and the heroine became one. In the human world, the couple faced the world together. They held their own views like they were opponents playing chess, and at the same time, they created a world for two.

Even I felt envious, so maybe some readers will envy them because of their love and their good life. They were discovered by the other characters in the book. Their love was exposed, and their feelings were tested.

The story, at this point, suddenly focused on the heroine's secret story; for example, where she went every day, if she saw her love, and her favorite things. She missed him every day, but she did nothing about it. She imagined he would take the initiative to contact her. Her object of secret love had moved away to another city. Her feelings were also revealed at this time. How did she spend her youth? As a female clerk, she observed, disdained, and criticized the relationships between young men and women, and she hid her feelings. Finally, one day she admitted to her elder colleague that she was deeply in love and was unable to extricate herself; the man, however, had moved to another city. She confided her heart to the elderly female clerk because she could not bear the loss.

"But you didn't take action." Her elder friend reminded her that she hadn't had social education. Her point of view was, "The actual action is real."

This heroine suddenly understood. It turned out that she had been living in chaos for a long time, and she didn't realize it. Then the heroine began to form her own opinions and even said, "Anything that has nothing to do with me does not exist."

Chapter 14

The next day I called and asked a chain furniture company if they could help to transport the special furniture on their website and deliver it to where I lived.

So, taking a day off, I went to this a large, two-story furniture store, which was located close to the city center, on a tree-lined avenue.

I walked in and took a shopping cart, like at a supermarket. I first came to some displays of decorated compartments, one by one, showing different functional uses, which inspired me. In addition to arranging my new home, the studio needs new furniture, such as what I saw—a computer desk and chair, placed in the studio, will give it a new appearance; of course, the simple the studio currently has is also very good.

A sales clerk was standing in front of a computer. A sales clerk also stood by the display of the sample furniture spaces, which was convenient for inquiring about the items, product models, and orders.

So I asked him for help. "Hello. Could you help me find these products?" I took out the list of the products I'd found on the webpage. Because I'd already checked through the webpage, the clerk only needed to order the styles of the sofa and bed frame that I wanted.

"Take this order and go first to the cashier to pay the bill," the clerk instructed me. "Then then take the receipt from the cashier to the shipping counter and hand it over to the clerk there, who will help you arrange the shipping service."

Everything was so simple and well planned, and the process was smooth-moving. No wonder, there were so many guests in this furniture store.

He quickly helped me choose the goods I wanted to buy. Then, I went to the checkout counter, like in a supermarket. A lot of people were in line at the checkout. I got out my credit card. I planned to pay by credit-card installments.

I walked out of the furniture store and looked for the nearest subway.

A few days later, I received a call on my cellular phone. It was the delivery people, who informed me that they were going to deliver my goods in the morning.

I thought about it. I decided not to go to the studio in the morning but instead to stay in my new home.

The next day, at close to eleven o'clock, the deliveryman came. I opened the door of the building. After entering the elevator through the vestibule, which was decorated with chandeliers, I waited for him to take the furniture pieces into the elevator, one by one.

After going upstairs and entering my new house, he asked me where the furniture should be placed. I told him that the bed frame should be placed on the wall of the bedroom, near the window, and the sofa should be placed in the living room against the main wall.

He knelt down, opened the box, and assembled the furniture, using a pneumatic screwdriver. It took him maybe thirty minutes. Finally, the furniture was assembled and placed in the position I had indicated. The deliveryman gave me two receipts, and I signed them and thanked him.

At noon, I ate a little bit of lunch.

I went to the studio in the afternoon. I checked my answering machine, but there weren't any messages. I went online and searched for some home decorating items, such as carpets and blankets.

I suddenly thought of something—for these kinds of goods, I could go to a superstore near the new home and buy them there.

So I got offline.

Today was not busy, so I left the studio and went to the superstore. I bought not only the carpet and blankets, but also chair cushions. The pattern was very classical and elegant, embroidered with a rose pattern.

After returning home, I set up everything. Now I have to live here for a while. This is my new home.

In the morning, I went to the studio, turned on the computer, and opened our studio's Facebook page, which allowed us to connect with many of the world's opera singers, opera houses, opera lovers, and friends. The former director in charge had set it up, and then it had been transferred to the account set up by the studio.

I saw lot of photos, messages, and news. The photos showed scenes after the show was finished, background scenes, or in the theater. There were also photos of the female stars and opera productions. Fans, friends, and opera lovers were in very intimate photos, very clever arrangements, so that the female soloist on the night of the show seemed warm-hearted.

There was a set of three photos of a great male singer that showed his stage presence. The photo had been shot from the top of the stage, looking down. He performed only with a piano accompaniment—it's not easy to perform in that style. In general, an untrained person or a member of a choir group who stands alone on stage will feel that his mind goes blank and often feels overwhelmed. People may even be nervous, and it is difficult to show their best sides, but this tenor in the photo was not nervous at all; he obviously was well-trained and had a rich stage experience.

Next there was a group of photos of the female star's performance on the stage. There were more than a dozen photos. She had three wardrobe changes throughout the show, and she worked with the orchestra and another male singer. The first photo showed her in a warm orange and pink dress with a long skirt with a long cloak of the same color. The next photo showed her in a low-cut black tulle dress with a long skirt. The dress made her look glamorous and sexy, her beautiful figure revealed through these costumes. The third photo showed her in a beaded-crystal vest with white yarn. The beautiful female star was pure elegance, and her temperament showed her elegant taste. She and the male singer sang a more popular musical tune, "Tonight."

This occasion, however, seemed to be at an informal concert hall, such as the arena, more like a pop singer's concert.

There also were some photos of recent stage operas during the opera season, as well as some that I had to guess what they were by the male and female protagonists' costumes and their expressions as they interpreted the opera scene? For example, one was the final scene of the first scene of the opera *Carmen*. The female protagonist, Carmen, tempted the officer, Don Jose. In the aria of the scene, she escaped, singing, "Pres des remparts de Seville" in Selvia, next to the old city wall.

There also was the role in the Verdi opera, *Ernani*, which recently was performed in Milan. They posted photos of the big chorus and the curtain call from the account of La Scala Opera House. It seemed that the main characters singers looked very happy in the photos, with the curtains pulled back on the stage. Congratulations to the lead vocal tenor, Francesco Meli. He has performed many roles in Verdi operas; for example, in the Verona area theater, he performed *Carmen* and *Un Ballo in Maschera*, and he recently performed the extremely high-level Verdi opera *Ernani* at La Scala Opera House. He has been on stage at La Scala Opera House, and his performances have attracted much attention. Opera fans may remember that the last famous cast member who performed *Ernani* at La Scala Opera House was Placido Domingo, but it was a performance in 1983, fifteen years ago. And the male lead tenor Meli was about to perform again in a work by the opera master Verdi, *Simon Boccanegra*. So the singer had recently performed and sung three roles by Verdi, including his important and famous role of his first performance.

Other photos were of concerts or a short section of an opera performance, which was fun and entertaining for opera lovers. I saw some photos taken in a studio with a larger stage, and a photo of a singer's recording work. He was wearing casual dress—a white shirt, a vest, a pair of long trousers that look like jeans, and shoes. There was a bottle of Alpine mineral water on the shelf and a Steinway piano on a platform, played by a senior musician. This looked like they were recording an album of art songs. It seemed the two were discussing details. Another photo was of the soundboard often seen in a separate room in the studio, with the monitor screen.

I thought of the files I used to work with in the studio. I saw a collection of songs recorded for a project and a selection of arias, but I didn't find any follow-up information.

This studio looked great. It was not a recording room but a recording studio that was like a small stage environment. The piano was top-notch, as was the recording microphone. This equipment gave people a grand feeling. It seemed that this space was very comfortable, and the temperature and humidity were suitable for singing and recording.

I remembered another thing—recently a world-class singer had published a book. Her first book-signing ceremony was held in London. I went to Amazon's website to search for the title, but her book had not yet arrived on this platform. (Later it did.)

For my new home kitchen, I also spoke with the interior designer. Since I have to stay in the studio, he came to my studio in the afternoon and showed me some samples and photos. In fact, I planned to design the interior. Although I was not to be adept at designing, I was afraid of asking some layman questions. He provided a lot of design ideas for the kitchen space, with an elegant high table and a bar, a chandelier, high chairs, and other space for studying that included a bookshelf, bookcase, and desk. The wood texture he had chosen looked very warm and comfortable. I liked it very much, and I also noticed, in one series of photos, that he liked to use glass compartments—glass compartment bedroom, glass compartment study room; it was a glass compartment sandwich.

"What is the purpose of so many glass compartments?" I asked.

"You can increase the sense of space," he told me.

"It looks very fashionable."

I continue to look at these design photos, but I couldn't make up my mind. I chose to make a bar and a high table and chairs because they looked beautiful, very fashionable, and had a good texture. They all had a secret charm. I was so excited.

Also, the overall design made the space comfortable and warm. I analyzed it, and the material chosen and lighting made the overall feeling comfortable.

I also saw a design photo. If you design a low-level four-person seat behind the square-shaped table, you will enjoy it. Comfortable wooden tables, wooden chairs, and upholstery—it seems like we are going to some chic shops, and it is a pleasure.

This interior design studio is very special. It even shows me some photos of the work of renovation. The ground is still cement—there are some bricks, cement, and carts—so the renovation of the site is not yet complete. I had to admire this interior design studio.

Gradually, I also felt that the benefits of the glass compartment not only created a sense of space but also of natural light. In addition to glass, the glass compartment had a metal frame and a wooden window frame, and some of them are carved wood, showing different design styles.

I chose a square table and a wooden four-person seat; it looks very elegant. The designer measured the area and said that he wants to go back to the company to draw the design.

I thought that my new house could be completed in one month, and I couldn't help but be happy.

I think of the purposes of the studio. Among them is this: "Based on the consideration of human nature, the purpose is for creating a thematic article on human nature." And that means that from the perspective of human nature, the creation is based on humanity. This is a theme I derived and intend to discuss.

Chapter 15

One of the search results I found for "humanity" on the internet was from Firenze, Italy. In 1400, the fifteenth-century word for "humanism" was *L'umanesimo*. The source of this word is from the Latin *humanitas*. Humanity includes people who suffer from humiliation, misfortune, and depression. They were present in the environment at the time.

The crafts produced in the fifteenth century include architecture, sculpture, and murals. And the spotlight focus was on architecture in the fifteenth century. Italy was an art and culture capital, and among the artists was the famous Leonardo DaVinci (1452–1519). His entire life was dedicated to culture and arts and crafts. He had such spirit and perseverance, and artistic heritage is admirable.

I am also learning how to present such a spirit and the brilliance of humanity through literary records and different writing styles in an article to convey such a spirit.

The "humanism" of Firenze also influenced the next Renaissance, and this more directly points out the works of art of this period, the center of the creation of the works—*Centralità*—and its spirit of sacrifice. The sense of space that is expressed in a building is from the shape of an arched doors, horizontally side by side or straight side by side, forming a corridor or corridors in different shapes.

I remembered St. Peter's Square in Vatican City. There is a cloister that looks like a keyhole. The shape is spectacular, and the white cloister looks quite elegant. It seems to make sense for people, seeming to be the spirit of heaven and giving people that impression. The spirit of the work itself is the same.

This spirit is also the purpose of this studio.

I suddenly had a feeling. I really missed the days when I went abroad for business. I missed the illusion of my loved one in my fantasy. I thought of not a name but a nickname, just a way to call her.

I was thinking about my experience at that time, and all the experiences with her at that time, as recorded in my experience of her work. I forgot to say that she is a writer and had already published several books when I met her. Her book has her story. She is so unique in my eyes that while everyone still does not understand why are they living in this city, she decided to go to abroad and go on many journeys.

I remembered my experience at that time. I was alone on the journey. In fact, I also experienced Paris's Charles de Gaulle Airport on the way. I had never taken such a long flight. It took almost twenty-five hours to arrive in Rome. I write in my diary that it was a day of farewell. I left work and group activities. I arrived in Rome on my own. I didn't have any relatives. I could only use my mobile phone to send text messages to connect with friends from far away and report my situation.

I took the subway in Rome. On the subway, I heard a conversation, and I was surprised. by the story of four people's life experiences—two men and two women. I am hesitated. I was in the seat next to them, about to introduce myself, but I wondered if I should get off, remain still, or pretend nothing had happened for four adults with four different stories.

At that moment, I was alone and going to People's Square. I was thinking, *Maybe I can walk from People's Square to Piazza di Spagna*. Anyway, I am alone, and there was no sure destination.

I came out of the subway station, but I still didn't understand why the underground exit was crowded with a large group of people. When I stood outside, I also was part of a large group of people. The nearby streets spread to Venice Square. I heard that there was a parking lot nearby. There, the people picked up their tour bus.

That was my first day in Rome.

Now I think that I was there for no purpose, and I was walking alone in the street.

Now I have a legitimate job—to help publish a novel titled *Summer Dreams*, organize files, and plan new proposals.

Maybe I should appreciate her care for me and thank her for looking after me when I was alone and abroad.

Chapter 16

arlier today, I used my web browser to watch the "Bell Song" in Delibes's opera *Lakme*, sung by coloratura soprano.

A song sung by the heroine, Lakme, tells the story of a homeless Indian girl who saved a group of travelers in the forest. The best one among the travelers recognized her unexpectedly. This traveler was the son of the Indian god Brama Vishnu. In order to thank her for her kindness, he brought her back to heaven, where she lived a happy life.

Lyrics of "Bell Song" are as follows:

In the ancient country of India,
There is a place called Paria.
In this place of Paria,
There are many Mimosa,
In the city, there are many children,
They are on the street,
Looking around, they are free to move,
They are the children of Paria.

There is a girl,
She saw a group of travelers in the forest.
They are like merchants, camels carry goods,
They seem to have encountered difficulties,
The girl shakes the bell.

(Coloratura fragment)

The girl saved them,
There is a special good in the merchants.
He recognized the girl,
If she is homeless in the forest,
She is just a little girl,
Paria is her home.

After returning from that trip, I had a special feeling in my heart for the travelers on the trip, as if it was me or it will be me in the future, and the travelers' experience was also or would be my experience.

I had a plan a possible business trip, but the situation here seems to be difficult for me to leave.

I think of the definition of *home* in my heart and my desire for home. It seems that in this opera, poetry-like verses are used, and the words imply the desire for home and the travelers' feelings about going home.

It is also like the crowd I saw in the People's Square in Rome; they were about to go home.

I have lived alone for many years, and my heart has deeper and deeper longing for this. Even when I am here, I still continue to experience my journey.

I have to pray for the travelers on the trip. Once again, this feeling of eagerness to go home is stronger than I am. My dignity, my will, the wall in my heart, and the boundary is no longer able to resist my desire to return home. And my heart is still praying, expecting that I will have a day to go home.

In addition to thinking about this with my loved one, I also have a grandmother. She is the principal of a university. We are not close, perhaps because of the age gap and, I guess, because of her point of view or perspective. I can't be called a model of hard work, and in her position as an educator, maybe she is tired of seeing young students slacking off and being lazy and ignorant. Because I have a family relationship with her, my point of view is that what she needs are young teenagers (instead of me) who can be role models and focus on naturalism. There is a sense for my life, I guess. The relationship between my parents and her is very stressful, and it has led to relationship lately that is not close. After all, their personal points of view are different.

On that trip, I also came to the university. There was a subway station entrance opposite it. I crossed the road from a walkway next to a river and walked onto the campus along the river. There were ducks on the river. They weren't swan; they were ducks with white feathers. Swans look elegant.

It was a bit windy, but the weather was fine. I wore a white shirt with a dark-blue sweater and dark trousers.

I wandered in that small area. Suddenly, I needed to go to the toilet. Maybe it was because of the breakfast I'd eaten at the hotel—a lot of tomatoes, and omelet, buns, cheese, and orange juice.

I entered a row of buildings that appeared to be five stories high, looking for a toilet.

After I came out, I observed the terrain. This terrace was also like a wall. If I could cross it, I could enter the campus. I tried to find a door, but I was stopped by a lady.

I stepped away and went back to the hall of the building. It was behind a library reading room. I thought, *Should I go in, or should I leave?*

I saw a group of women standing in the middle of the hall, talking. They seemed to be the school's faculty. I thought, *Is my grandmother there?* However, we hadn't seen each other in a long time. I didn't know her hairstyle or style of dress, and this day is just one day in these many years.

Time was so short, and a thought that prompted me to leave: *Maybe all her efforts are spent on education.* Her dedication to her teaching has made it hard for me and other people in the family to stay connected. I stayed alone all day long—a traveler who travels alone. I can't stand that those who are together all day call each other friends and partners.

I thought of my relationship with my family. If they were so clearly separated from each other, then what kind of relationship could they have with other people or their descendants?

I thought of the longing in my heart, and I felt a sense of loss and a desire for home.

Chapter 17

$\mathcal{I}$ n the morning, I came to the studio, where I continued my work. It seemed I had a routine, and I had not yet made a new proposal.

I received my screen amplifier, and I researched this new product. I pulled the curtains, looked for a dark corner, set it up, and carefully moved the company's iPhone from behind the screen. On the left side, it slowly moved into the screen area.

I tested it, but the effect was not satisfactory. I played with it for a while and read the manual. I had never had the patience to read the manual—I had a bad habit of skipping that step. From the second illustration, I jumped to the description of the third item, and then I jumped back to the description of the first item.

After playing with it for a while, I was able to set it up correctly, but the angle of the phone and the screen still was not right, so I pulled up a chair and sat down to try it.

Next, I checked the computer and saw an email—an advertisement from an opera magazine, which mentioned the list of selected singers in the New Year's opera singing competition.

It was not easy to hold a singing competition every year. Many young men and women who are interested in opera performance are attracted to the opera field and participate in singing competitions. How long does it take? How much effort and spirit is spent in participating in such an event?

I was reminded of the former studio director. According to the old files left on the computer, he was very interested in performing opera singing and had learned some works. I think he was planning to go to Europe, maybe Germany, to record, but the recordings were in his personal collection and were not placed in the studio's archives.

I thought about how much magic or charm the opera has, and it makes some people almost desperate to invest in the field.

Although I never learned the Italian while at university, I can understand a little bit of the lyrics when I listen to opera music.

From the study of a language, to the study of the music, to the singing method of vocal music, to the ability to learn an entire opera, you could find favor in the theater, stand on the stage, and perform opera roles—but how hard it is!

This is really a long road to learning. Moreover, I suspect that this is mostly based on self-study, self-teaching, and memorizing a complete opera. The learner must be independent and hardworking and have a tireless learning spirit and perseverance.

I have a sense of exclusion on the stage. I don't like to feel someone is instigating me when I stand on stage and present a role. The aspect of opera that I like tends to relate to the feelings of my heart. This is also the essence of the aria.

To only to talk about a character in the opera and how to play it or the character's habits and faults or blind spots will only make me lose interest in an opera.

I saw a small box in the screen magnifier package; I thought it was an attachment. When I opened it, it turned out to be a small Bluetooth speaker. The small shape is quite cute, and it is equipped with a neon-light flashing device. The development of modern technology in these small electronic products, is really interesting.

I picked up the company's iPhone, turned on the Bluetooth receiver's control button, searched for a web radio station from the Apple Music app, and immediately listened to it. The content was in my music app under "My Favorites." In the beginning was a duet, followed by the duet in the second act of *Andrea Chenier*. When I heard that, the hair on my arms stood on end, and it was followed by the duet in *Aida*, which was a work of heroic style.

I remembered another thing about the theme—the main theme of some heroic operas, or the heroes and heroines. What are the heroes in the eyes of opera fans? In the drama *Andrea Chenier*, Andrea, because of the emotional relationship in the complicated plot of the story, chose to die at the end of the play, and that moved the heroine, Maddalena, to go to the execution ground with him. In the plot of the story, with its revolutionary thought or concept, and it the point of view of the audience, the protagonist could be called a hero. The audience must identify with a character or an actor, and two aspects that need to be explored. Should the opera be interpreted according to the plot, which depends on the director's actions, or should it be the will of the character? This is a topic for research and discussion.

I think of Delibes's *Lakme*. In this story, does Lakme like the British officer Gerald? From the beginning of the story, Lakme had a good impression on him. His father rejected the British officers who joined the British army to enter India, and then we learn that Gerald is captured. At the end of the play, Lakme gives water to Gerald and lets go. Lakme lives in an ancient civilization of India; this is her love story. She is an Indian girl who has rebelled against her homeland, and the audience that favors Gerald would be touched by her. The good deed of reciprocation could also be well regarded, as could be the person who dares to do it. For the story of the opera and its educational significance, it is often built into the background of such a story. The protagonist is deeply immersed in such a situation, and in the dilemma, he still maintains his own will. He is criticized by the people around him, but he still is unyielding and overcomes the situation with perseverance, by himself.

A similar role is Aida in *Aida*, from the aria of the third act: "Oh, patria mia" (or "Oh, my hometown") is heard. It's the heroine's desire for her hometown.

In *Lakme*, the aria of Lakme, "Bell Song," tells the story of the orphan girl in Paria. The audience feels empathy in the way the story is told.

I have observed that some opera fans are fascinated by operas and characters in the drama, and they even envy. In reality, what the characters of these stories need is sympathy.

That may be the climax of the plot and the essence of the opera.

Chapter 18

I want to cultivate a little emotional appeal. I plan to make Italian dishes in the kitchen of my new home.

The square counter that I selected is also practical, but for the dining set, the designer suggested that I choose a lighter, European-style dining table and chair. I think the style is elegant, and the price is fairly affordable. I agreed with his suggestions.

I went to the supermarket to buy food. Today was not sunny. There were not many customers in the supermarket, and there were no special imported goods.

I decided to make *a pasta alle vongole* (or spaghetti with clams) that I'd had in Italy. Here, I saw a very good sale on clams. They seemed to be cheap, big and fat. I'd thought they were only good enough for ginger soup. It piqued my interest.

I came to the noodle area, where there are many dried noodles, shell noodles, spaghetti, Chinese noodles, etc. I finally found the Italian noodles, which were darker in color and seemed thicker. I studied the noodles to see if they were bucatini—a noodle with a hollow center.

Next, I went to the freezer to buy ice cream bars, and I also bought seasoning ingredients, garlic, and rosemary.

I eat a lot of snacks and don't often cook for myself. If I'm busy at work, I usually prepare a meal in three to five minutes. The quality of the food and time spent eating are not good.

I have learned the names of many Italian dishes, such as various Italian pasta, *formaggio* (cheese), *dolce* (sweet), and so on. The cooking teacher's attitude is to teach the name of the Italian dish as well as how to prepare it.

There is a foreign population in Italy, about a quarter of the population. In recent years, there has been an increasing trend, for social and health reasons, toward the so-called "slow food movement," which promotes maintaining a good mood during eating and to eat without being hurried.

A formal lunch of Italian cuisine should contain antipasti, the first course, the second course, the dessert, and the drink. As the customers start to eat the first dish, the waiter will call out, "Buon appetito!" or "Enjoy your meal!"

I went home, boiled the water, threw in the washed clams, and sprinkled in some salt. I also added some slices of garlic and rosemary.

In another pot, I boiled water added noodles.

The boiling water for the clams was getting less and less. It looked like a souse. I would turn off the burner and drain the souse.

The other noodles were boiled, drained, and placed on a beautifully shaped plate. Then I topped them with broth.

Today, I made an exception and opened a bottle of sparkling fruit wine I'd bought at the supermarket. I had decided to stop drinking for two years, but the taste of this bubble drink can simulate champagne.

At the supermarket bakery, I bought the dessert tiramisu. Because it was from a bakery, the portion was quite generous.

The above was my lunch today.

I came to the studio in the morning and opened the email box. There were two new emails. One was an advertisement for four writers with their newly published books. Testimonials were published through a website. The theme of each of the four books was different. One was a historical fantasy novel about a empire age—a princess's love story. Another told a lawyer's story from the viewpoint of the legal department's interns. They learned to rely on their own efforts to overcome the difficulties they experienced while working in the law office. There also was a modern novel about a young woman in the fashion industry and how she chose between work and life. The fourth book was a motivational book that dealt with the difficulties encountered in postmodern people's lives and how to recognize the problem, solve it, and live a leisurely modern life.

These books might appeal to avid readers, I thought.

I have to be convinced in my heart that the books the publishing house chooses to publish are the type that modern readers want to read. It is no wonder that many people now only buy books from the internet. Through this channel, they can easily find the topics they are interested in. I am amazed that I often can't find a book on a topic that interests me in a chain bookstore. However, it is different when looking through webpage advertisements. These will tell you a little bit of the story content to pique reader interest. After the reader's sees a bit of the book, a book that might not have seemed too promising now induces interest. It has hooked the reader; this is the pleasure of reading.

I recently had read *Summer Dreams*. Now I thought about how to write about the story to interest readers and so that this book also would seem attractive.

I wrote:

> In the morning, he walked on the same path and went to a coffee shop. His life was the same as usual. He did the same job all the time, but no one noticed him until she appeared, and that freed him from his suffocating life. They appreciated each other's beauty …

I felt a smile in my heart; then I translated the above into French to see how it felt.

I thought, *Maybe I should send this blurb to the editor. Then again, if the publisher has four books to publish and advertise every day, maybe the editor won't have time to read it.*

I thought of the special features of *Summer Dreams*, perhaps not only its love story, but also its answers to the dilemmas of life. It created a model; people who are overwhelmed by life have a choice to live like the characters in the novel.

I thought for a long time and decided that in addition to the above-mentioned features, *Summer Dreams* had a special feature. The story showed sympathy for women and gave a deep description of the male protagonist's situation.

In general, most love stories are based on the description of women's encounters. It is rare to use men as the starting point. Not many people know of this dilemma in society.

Sometimes, I am also deeply sympathetic to orphans. If this was a story about an orphan, the description of the dilemma he encountered during his growing up years makes my description of the story more intense.

Looking back, however, how much sympathy could this society give to a young man or an orphan? Could they sympathize with him? If a pair of men in real life who encountered the same situation could not sympathize with each other, then could a man who educated an adult in a normal setting sympathize with an orphan?

The author caused the reader to have preconceived notions, thinking that the hero was good, until halfway through the story. Then the heroine enters his life, everything is exposed—for example his life, his family background—and it turns out that his uniqueness is part of his unique way of life.

There is also another way of writing. The male character in the story is always unwilling to reveal it. The true feelings in his heart are not expressed throughout the complicated plot, creating the setup for the climax.

In the postmodern way of life, it is difficult for me to admire and sympathize with the piteous of the world. However, the pain of losing loved ones still cannot change the situation or degree of sorrow. People who are deaf and lost must still have the care of others. Even in the postmodern society, people still have difficulty in getting their pain out of their own strength.

I was born with a feeling that seems like loving the house itself.

I think about the hero of the story—alone, quietly walking down the street. If no one sympathizes with him, how miserable will his fate be? And among the people he's met, isn't theirs a fate similar to his—or even more tragic?

The voice of resistance is still there, and some people still refuse to feel sympathy for such an encounter. Where is the crux of the problem?

Is this resistance derived from prejudice or other reasons? The idea that some people have preconceived notions is so deep-rooted that they are like the roots of strong trees. They are unbreakable. They grow every day, and they become like cages. In such a cage, could a prisoner come out from the inside and get rid of its control?

Such a lack of sympathy and stifling environment make the male and female protagonists in the story deeply trapped in the trap of love. Just like in winter, when the trees are bare, it is not enough to express people's indifference until the snowstorm. The day that came, and the people in the story—as well as the readers—learned that the coldness of nature is colder and more terrible than the hearts of people, as if to destroy this environment.

In this case, for a few weeks, the protagonist in the story, in addition to suffering from fate, is bound by his environment.

It's cold winter, and the summer when they met seems like a different time and space—like two things that are completely irrelevant, as if this is another environment, another story. Love and enthusiasm are completely gone; only the cold is the normal state.

I have studied a little bit about post-traumatic stress syndrome. For the trauma that is encountered in a moment, people adopt an attitude of not believing or accepting it, so that the shock they encounter in an instant can be explained. However, if this wound does not heal, it will exist in a person's heart for a long time. Although it is buried very well, after a time, it can't bear a new blow, and it is irreparable.

I studied the characters in the story. Perhaps he was in such a situation and could not extricate himself.

I am like a bystander, but inevitably, I fall into the same situation that the protagonist has encountered.

I then closed the book and closed my eyes. I tried to no longer thinking about it, to no longer think about the hero of this story, his psychological issues, or his being hit by such a big blow.

I realized that he also refused to mention something, which made me stop, as if we could not associate with our friends.

Chapter 19

*I*t was a rainy day, so I came to the studio with an umbrella. The whole atmosphere was a rainy day. I wanted to buy a cup of coffee, but because it was raining, I was too lazy to go out. Also, I found that coffee affects the spirit and my sleep. At my old age, I have to start paying attention and maybe go from five cups of coffee a week to two or three cups of coffee a week.

When I traveled to Italy, espresso was sold in a small cup that was only as large as a container of creamer, which also caused a miscalculation of research. The black coffee, which sells very well here, is generously sold in mugs, and the research report we read in the newspaper might use a different amount for a cup. My observations show that Europeans are more cautious about drinking coffee. Unlike coffee shops here, they treat coffee as a drink, and they drink it in a large cup, completely ignoring its possible impact and the side effects it causes.

I am looking for a substitute drink. That is the black tea I bought at my breakfast shop. After reading *Summer Dreams*, I learned that the hero in the story would drink a cup of black tea with his breakfast in the morning.

Not only in the morning, but sometimes when I go to a beverage store that sells black tea, I drink it. I like its color—deep red, with a little reddish brown, some even black—plus a lot of syrup. Maybe I like the sweetness of black tea, not the black tea itself. Of course, the tea is very fragrant. It is also the reason for the popularity of black tea, but black tea is too ordinary. The black tea in the breakfast shop comes with a fructose syrup, instead of the maple syrup produced in Canada or Europe.

I used to work in a department store that had a coffee machine, and the special thing was that the sweetener it used was maple syrup. I brewed a cup of coffee, cooled it, and then added maple syrup from the refrigerator. The whole cup of coffee was cold, and this became my favorite drink in summer.

When I was young, I would drink coffee, but I didn't feel it at the time or realize the seriousness health effects. In addition to the probability of osteoporosis, I think there is still a problem, and that is a sleep problem. Sometimes, when I lost sleep the night before, the next day I had to go to the coffee shop and buy a cup of coffee, so that I could take a nap, or I wouldn't get a good night's sleep.

In addition to the problem of caffeine in the coffee, there is also the problem of sugar intake. Some people drink coffee and add four to five packets of sugar to a cup, which also causes problems with illness. Some obese patients should not use such a large number of sugar packets when drinking coffee.

Some coffee lovers equate coffee with noble tastes. Indeed, coffee does promote our lives to another spiritual level, but we should not forget to carefully manage our lives and master the planning. Taking care of the details of important things can make us more aware of the true meaning of life. Perhaps some people who are good at recording the events in their lives are more likely to appreciate everything in life.

In the afternoon, I entered the studio and opened the Facebook studio account. As I've said, there are many current opera performances or concert news on the studio account.

Today, I saw a dynamic short film of a beautiful tenor, a short film that is about to be in theaters in the United States. It was filmed in the center of the opera house. The theater is beautiful. You can see the boxes on both sides and the giant chandeliers. The overall color and texture of the fabrics in the theater are red velvet and gold, with golden lights.

I remembered a similar production this tenor had held in Irlanda a few days ago. He was accompanied by an orchestra and sang an aria. The songs included the aria "Celeste Aida," from the first act of Aida, and songs from the second act of *Carmen*. He also sang "Song of

Flowers" and two arias from Puccini's *Tosca*, the second of which was an encore.

His seemed to be an easygoing person, and the short film was enjoyable. He seemed in good spirits and friendly, and these tracks show his considerable stage performance experience.

The live performance on the stage has an instant, even impromptu effect, and his voice is so grand and bright, with a penetrating power—a grand volume with a warm temperament, like a bright copper pipe fitting into an orchestra. Although the tone is warm and fascinating, it still has penetrating power. He probably was the tenor who was the biggest hit in recent years.

For the voices, such as the tenor, you can divide the details into the early contralto, the Mozart-style lyric tenor, until the recent heroic tenor. The tenor's voice is both lyrical and heroic. He previously sang Mozart's opera works, followed by Verdi's works, such as *Rigoletto, Un Ballo in Maschera*, and so on.

Continuing to browse, I came across information that indicated *La Traviata* would premiere in the opera season of New York's Metropolitan Opera in 2018–19.

I remembered a call I'd received a few days ago from a person who claimed to be the head of the former studio. He knew that the studio had a music data collection. He wanted to visit and view what might be precious collections.

When he came to see it, I told him that the studio's collection of the classic operas from 1970 to 1980 was the most complete. In the 1960s, their recording quality was too old or of varying quality. The most recent was the electronic MP-3 file, which could be read and listened to using the Apple Music app. Most of them had been recorded in 1990 and later in the millennium.

After he had looked and listened for a long time, he still seemed to have a hard time, and finally asked, "Could I borrow this version of Verdi's *La Traviata*?"

I thought he might want to look back at the time of that era; after all, this recording had been around a long time, nearly forty years. I introduced some of the more recent recordings of the same drama.

He thought about it and then told me that he was a fan. He had an old recording, but he wanted to hear it—the reprint of the studio's collection—to see if it was different.

He seemed careful and polite, and he was very interested in audio recordings. He also strongly recommended to me this singing cast, which was his first choice for this drama.

He was a true opera fan.

After he left, I thought about it. In today's busy opera world, for some older fans, how did they make the choice of a new production of the opera, when they had the classic recordings in mind.

I was reminded of how these deeply rooted and established impressions impacted the current opera world—the same rehearsal and staging, but the opera fans get the most beautiful impression, left in that era, the enviable era. What secret magic is there, so that people do not forget?

Next, I browsed freely and saw a senior fan of opera. He shared his hobby of opera on Facebook. He said that he lives in music every day— he walks, works, goes to the gym, and in his mind and in his heart, the music supports him and encourages him. His favorite pastime is music. Moreover, it is actually opera. When he listens to it, he can enjoy himself and enjoy his life. This is his own way of life.

I think that in the postmodern era, the media is developed and flooded with news and information. There are still many people who scream that life is boring and empty. Still, it is impossible to find the joy of life from media, videos, and recordings.

A classical music fan describes his own way to enjoy his life, that it is to be treasured.

If you have never recognized what is worth living in, you will never live.

Perhaps postmodern people are still too busy, but they need to be educated, reviewing the life they have had and making life more fun.

I was reminded of a video of the opera appreciation last year, a summary of the recordings, and my review. I also recalled my original intention for doing so.

Perhaps the Philharmonic is another realm in which I am just living.

(The opera diva said, "If you sincerely realize my feelings, I'll sincerely sing for you.")

In the morning, when I reviewed the novel *Summer Dreams*, I read the paragraph below:

> Look at those people who tell their readers about their unfortunate backgrounds and encounters. Some have lost their marriage, some have passed away, some have single-parent families, and some have physical illnesses. When my story mentions their unfortunate encounter, it originally was meant to cause sympathy. Why was that not their first reaction; rather, it was resentment and disgust. They should not be sad. Seek comfort. Some people think of them, taking into account their feelings and unfortunate encounters? Why?

I read this and thought about the same problem in my heart.

The suffering people, eager to get comfort, have to tell others of the hardships of their hearts, but they are worried that they will hear their unfortunate experiences talked about by other people.

This pain has caused a contradiction.

Therefore, some people choose not to talk about themselves, but if they are alone, they will eventually break.

I think of myself and the people who have encountered these misfortunes. Although we do not have an intersection in real life, the sources of pain are similar.

The melody began again, and a voice was heard in my heart. It seems that after these days, it is rooted in my heart. How will it affect my life?

Some helpless, unwilling, and unsolvable things and encounters are like a play, like we still see those who are unfeeling, because at that time, people still don't understand that is their own story.

I am reminded of many touching stories—a mother whose marriage is weak, a girl who has lost her parents, an adopted orphan. They, one by one, appear in this melody, and then disappear.

I suddenly thought that it was a valuable thing to have a person in one's life who can be a trusted partner.

I also remembered the male and female protagonists in the story of *Andrea Chenier*, the environment they were in, and the things they encountered. On that night when they finally met and lived forever, they lived for love. The people around them wanted them to die, so they chose to die together and calmly. The hardships of suffering for love were gone, and their love surpassed all the obstacles.

"If you have cared about me—my situation, my experience—even if it is only a second, for a moment, then you have loved me."

"If we say that fate has caused many hardships to my family and my life, then it is the same with you. We are sympathetic to each other."

"If I say that I will lose my fate and be executed, I am still willing to guard your heart."

"So, if so, I will choose to go to die with you, and I will not live alone."

"Yes, go to death together."

"Yes, go to death together."

"If people want to prove that the value of love is going to die, I have to prove that it is better to die together."

("It doesn't have to be so urgent.")

Yes, together.

Chapter 20

I thought of a proposal for a language travel book for the studio, *Travel around Roma, and Speak Italian.* In addition to sightseeing and language, the publisher is also interested in other languages, such as Spanish and German—and the project was made. The series of books was *Travel around Berlin, and Speak German, Travel around Madrid, and Speak Spanish*, and so on.

Being able to work with a publisher, providing and producing useful books and introducing them to the public, was a really rewarding job.

After finishing the studio's recent plans, for the next two or three months, my work will focus on the following:

1. The routine work of the studio
2. Taking a private tutoring class—preparation and review
3. Studying the original textbook of a singing technique
4. Planning a new proposal for myself

I took out the iPhone and distributed a timeline as follows:

In the morning
9:00–10:20
10:30–11:30

Lunchtime

1:40–2:30 p.m.
2:40–3:30
3:40–4:30
4:40–5:30

Then, by assigning these items to the timetable, I could adjust it flexibly. For example, in the morning, sometimes I come to the studio at seven o'clock, or there is not so much work in the afternoon. I can flexibly use the third and the first time slots, leave the studio early, go shopping, or prepare some studio daily necessities or consumables.

Maybe the focus is on the morning, or the first and second time slots of the afternoon. These activities are also matched with some of the activities I will do in my daily life, such as drinking a cup of coffee, eating fruit for the vitamins my body needs, browsing the internet, or collecting some information, pictures, videos, or music files.

I also noticed that I couldn't take any time to review the contents of my tutoring class. Now, I will plan to improve this situation and go to the library to review. Perhaps the studio or the new home environment is not suitable. The environment of the library's study room is more suitable for reviewing textbooks.

I am hesitating about one thing. If the work of the American publishing house requires a paragraph, I can plan the difference. Maybe I could think of a new proposal in my journey. However, I am still waiting for the latest news from New York, so the plan has to be shelved.

All these plans must be suspended while I wait for the US company to have a formal response, in order to have follow-up plans.

During this period, *Summer Dreams* received a good response from readers. I heard that seven thousand copies of the first wave of trials in New York were sold out. I still looked forward to a good response from other cities in the United States.

I said that this novel should have been written by the former director of studio. I participated in the English manuscript and assisted in the publication of the English version. I am very grateful to him for creating this studio. I just regret that he left. He was as not able to wait until this time when I was able to personally receive good news from the United States. My heart is silently praying that this novel can become a best-seller. That would be a meaningful thing. The preface in the book mentioned that he thanked those people around him for making him a love story like this, even though this novel story is not 100 percent perfect. In the end, it is a good way to teach people, one lesson being that the weakness of the blow suffered by the protagonist shows that this character is alive, human, and flesh-and-blood.

I changed my original business trip plan and will not go abroad for a while. I will study more about the interviews in this book and also record today as a special, celebrated day.

In the evening, I returned to my new home. I took a bottle of sparkling water—champagne flavor—and a box of white chocolate. I planned to celebrate. I should be glad that I have not traveled abroad, as I received this exciting news here.

I washed a glass, shook the sparkling water bottle, opened it, and watched it spurt foam, as if it was my heart. I sat on a red sofa, eating chocolate, and drinking a sparkling drink.

I thought about one of the proposals in my plan, about singing skills. How could I make it interesting and in line with the public's taste?

I looked out the window and thought about an old song, a story about the birth of Bethlehem's baby.

I picked up my phone, checked my text messages, and saw I had one from Sofia.

"Please remember to reply to the publisher's email about the market survey tomorrow."

Sofia is the new assistant who came to the trial last week to help me with some chores so I could start new projects and proposals.

Sofia was of medium build, with fair skin, and short black hair. She always wears pink lipstick. When she came to the interview, her black pantsuit was impressive.

She had to leave college because of family and career planning, but she will go back to school to make up the credits. The studio is looking for a work-study student. After I evaluated it, I thought, *Maybe a high school graduate student is better than Sofia, who has already taken credits at the university. Sofia has a better situation.*

Unfortunately, she only met the requirements during the trial period. I expected people I could fully trust. There was still a distance to go, but there must be a beginning to everything.

Regarding replying to the publisher's email, I can wait until tomorrow morning.

I turned on my bedside CD player and chose a CD of German lieder that I recently bought on Amazon. I imagined the cold climate of Europe, of Germany at this time, compared with the warmth and comfort here. How lucky are the residents here?

The climate of the earth, which is commonly known as the "extreme earthquake" phenomenon, gradually divorced itself from the warm and hot climate of summer in the Northern Hemisphere, showing another look. In nature, plants' leaves turn red or yellow, more capably expressed in this atmosphere.

The summer described in *Summer Dreams* seems a long time ago.

That morning, Sofia sent an email. Because she is a part-time reader, she doesn't have to stay in the studio. The email she sent was a short message:

> Hello. See what I found from the archives. It's a missing proposal from the studio, "The First Approach to a Legendary Novel." Read it.
> Have a good day!
> —Sofia

I'd read the proposal of "The First Approach to a Legendary Novel" when I first came to the studio to organize the files. However, the result of my research was that most of the files had been lost. I read it a bit and the story it tells. It is about an opera diva, but her real name and the many names she is called are no longer acceptable.

But the wonderful thing is that there are some parts of these documents that seem to be recorded in the form of diaries. Who was the original author? And why does he have such understanding and a clear interpretation of the opera diva and her time? Where does its source come from? Or where does its inspiration come from?

Its contents are attached to the catalogue, as follows, but some have only a title, and the text is not available:

1. After the "The First Approach to a Legendary Novel"
2. Talking about the life of the opera diva
3. Talking from the Chinese Dragon Boat Festival culture about Western opera
4. The opera diva in the era of performing *Andrea Chenier*
5. The death of the opera diva
6. Phoenix Opera House in Venice
7. Italian ribbon
8. The heyday of the opera of the 1960s
9. Come to Naples
10. Searching for the emotional life of the operatic diva from *Lucia*

Topic: "Talking from the Chinese Dragon Boat Festival Culture about Western Opera"

The end of May brings the Dragon Boat Festival in China. It is one of the three Chinese festivals. In traditional folklore, the legend of Bai Niang-Niang tells the story of Mr. Tsu Xian, a scholar of Chinese ordinary people. In the West Lake, the embodiment of the avatar has been cultivated into white-and-green two-demon snakes. The pseudonyms are Bai Su-Zheng and Xiao-Ching, and with Tsu Xian, they will become a husband and wife and save the local people in peril, but Bai Su-Zheng is pregnant with Tsu Xian's child. They are the second generation of Tsu Shi-Lin, the abbot of the Fa-Hai, whose temple is called the Fa-Guan, and finally, Bai Su-Zheng is found under the pagoda Lei-Fon on the side of West Lake. That is legendary story in Chinese.

In the legendary novels, stories about people and nonhuman love, or stories of love and hate in the nonhuman world, are adapted into opera stories, such as Devzark's opera *Lusaka* (aka *Mermaid Princess*) or Wagner's full-length opera, *The Ring of Nibelungen*, which tells the story of the love and hate of the gods, the fairy world, the world, and the underworld.

Among them are "Valkyrie" and later, "Siegfried," the most popular, who tells the female Valkyrie Brunnhilde, who was frozen by Vulcan Wotan, to avoid the entanglement between the fairyland and the world. And in "Siegfried," Siegfried rescued Brunnhilde from the ice and fell in love with her.

However, Brunnhilde listened to the warnings of Vulcan Wotan before the ice froze, and she experienced the years of ice. Brunnhilde's youthful appearance remained the same, but she was cursed. She used a dagger to stab Siegfried from behind to avoid Siegfried's sitting on the throne, bringing misfortune to the world.

Also, in Mendelssohn's musical *A Midsummer Night's Dream*, after a spell is cast, the protagonist falls in love with a donkey on the evening of midsummer's night until magic broke the spell.

In another Wagner opera, *The Flying Dutchman*, the heroine, Senta, falls in love with the ghost captain. Between the father of the family and the fiancé's dilemma, she finally is sacrificed in the end the story of lyricism.

The mythological drama has come out of the common sense of the world and has become a kind of adjustment for life.

When watching the mythological drama and listening to the music, you must be careful not to transcend the boundaries between humans and God and the common sense of the world.

Verdi's opera does not talk about the love between people, ghosts, and immortals but shows it as a kind of metaphor. For example, during the dance of the witch in the first scene of the opera *Macbeth*, the second scene of the second act, the ghosts of the dead Banco and King Duncan appear, and the forest outside the castle moves in the third scene. There are many musical elements in the middle—for example, dance music, drinking songs, and military songs—giving a very lively depiction of Shakespeare's plays.

Tracing back, during the period of the bel canto opera, there was a story of Donizetti, *Lucia di Lammermoor*. In the first scene, Lucia told the waitress, Alissa, about the reflection of the woman in the fountain in the garden. In the second scene of the second act, there is the "wedding signing." And the "mad scene" appears at the end of the third act. Lucia is covered in blood, wearing a white dress and playing with a knife. The orchestra flute plays the theme of a dominant motive, just like a lively realism scene. In the absence of human logic, music plays an important role here. Listening to music, with a small amount of written language, simple statements, or even just sighs, constitutes a surreal scene. When there are many people, they always say too much, and the opera *Lucia di Lammermoor* provides a good time. A great scene, completely played by the heroine, Lucia, without restraint, as if in the baroque period, made a revolutionary difference.

In the era of the Baroque, the characters are simple. The content is mostly arias of purity, and in this period of the melody opera, the composer—for example, Bellini, Donizetti, and so on—pays more attention to the performance level of the opera than the drama that's presented, not only the singing of the song but also the effect of the drama of the performance. Lucia takes this characteristic to the extreme, like the storyteller in the drama. In the drama, Lucia performs as a storyteller, and she is in love with the hero, Edgardo, but they cannot get together. Aria and scene interpretation tell of their love. The story of the opera *Lucia di Lammermoor*, a bel canto opera drama, has become a landmark and beyond reality.

For the part of Edgardo, the lead actor, at the end of the third act, there was nearly twenty minutes of solo and chorus lead singers. The finale of the show, especially the ending aria—"We will reunite in heaven (in the name of heaven)" ("ne congiunga il nume in ciel")—makes the story sublimate to the metaphysical beauty. It's the best echo and explanation for Lucia's "mad scene," making this drama a romantic love tragedy, increasing the feeling of grief that is not pleasing but that is more likely to resonate and reverberate.

Recently, I listened to the live broadcast of *Lucia di Lammermoor* from the Bologna City Opera on the Italian radio station Rai 3. It ended with the aria of the lyric tenor, live broadcast from the scene. The performance has achieved unprecedented success. Despite the quality of the live radio and the enthusiastic response of the theater audience, the time difference between Italy and this city is six hours. By the end of the drama, it was already four o'clock here. If the Philharmonic fans are ignoring the daytime, I don't know if there will be a time difference or a sense of time and space. Compared with the Edgardo of the predecessors, such as primo tenor Luciano Pavarotti, the inheritance of the opera world and the enthusiasm of the opera fans could be seen.

The production of opera, under the constraints of human nature and timely and empty background, emphasizes rhythm, efficiency, and economy, and that could best show the essence of the opera. As the opera goddess diva Maria Callas once said, "The audience sees only the excerpts."

Music Appreciation

1. Wagner's *Valkyrie*—the flight of Valkyrie
2. Verdi's *Nabucco*—riding the wings of thought
3. Gounod's *Mireille*—the end of the second act
4. Berlioz's *Mefestole*—Mefestole's aria
5. Mascagni's *Cavelleria Rusticana*—intermezzo between acts II and III

Chapter 21

Topic: "The Opera Diva During the Rehearsal of *Andrea Chenier*"

I think of my memoirs of the opera diva. In this time, in France, how did she spend the day? The people around her are not as friendly as they were before in the opera world. Some of them were dead, and some escaped. And that is not originally the opera world she entered anymore. The aura of the world that she entered first is no longer, which was the aura given to her by her godfather. People around her are full of hopelessness. They have chosen their lives. They can choose not to do like this and instead choose mutual help. But they are not willing. They are not willing to choose to live. The feeling is indifference, raising the wall of the martyrdom between them, and thus becoming the curse of their destiny.

The rehearsal of the opera *Andrea Chenier* begins under such circumstances.

Giordano's opera *Andrea Chenier* is a love story between the heroine, Maddalena, and the hero, Andrea Chenier, during the French Revolution in 1789. Because the background is revolutionary, the so-called "story of the great era" is different from other operas. For example, the love story, in the form of novel narrative, adds a background to the revolutionary period and looks at the young people's sentiments in that period from the perspective of opera music.

At that time, the environment, the corrupt society, the people living in the wrong place, were not tolerant of the aristocrats' daily pampering, and masses protested on the streets. The relationship between the people in Paris and the authorities was seriously strained. There was a feeling of "How can we abandon humanity?" But they were eager for the aura of humanity, so full of contradiction in reality.

After the outbreak of the French Revolution in 1789, the story comes to the aristocratic home of the heroine, Maddalena. In this drama, for the opening music, the servants are busy, everyone is busy, under a pleasant atmosphere, and everything seemed prosperous—a gratifying sight. That's because today, a group of VIPs are coming. In the process of waiting and preparing, the ladies expectations are full of dreams and some embarrassment, because the knight Andrea Chenier, who Maddalena admires, is also among the guests. Maddalena is happy along with everyone, but they do not know her story, her life, and this scene today is a prelude. From then on, she and Andrea will become the sole figures in their lives, completing a French love story after the outbreak of the French Revolution. Regrettably, this story does not finish with marriage in the end but with the tragedy of the male and female protagonists, who went to the execution ground together and lost their heads.

Maddalena was a naive girl, but she might also have sensed the revolutionary aura of her surroundings. How can she be so lucky and have a happy life?

The guests arrived at the mansion. The first scene was in a living room. The scenes are of meeting with friends and relatives, feeling the warmth of the people, and everyone having a good time. With piano accompaniment, the knight Andrea is invited to share an impromptu poem: "A blue clear sky among them …" ("Un di all'azzuro spazio …").

> Un di all'azzuro spazio
> Guardai profondo,
> e ai prati colmi di viole,
> Pioveva loro I'll sole,
> e folgorava d'oro il mondo …

The poem sings of his enthusiasm for the motherland, but the background and atmosphere of the Revolution are reminiscent of the knight's, a patriotic poet's, dissatisfaction with the political situation and his ambition, full of reform.

Andrea turns to Maddalena, making Maddalena's eyes more melancholy.

Back in the French Revolution, the environment at that time held such disappointment and hopelessness. In this case, what can people rely on for Maddalena's life? Life is not guaranteed. How can Maddalena have any expectations for love?

The third act describes that Andrea was arrested by the authorities because of the tension. Maddalena went to the court's secretary, Gerard, to plead with the shame of a servant in act I. She sang the famous aria of the play, "La mamma morta." This aria is a change in her life. Her character has moved in one direction, and that is toward death. As far as Maddalena and her mother are concerned, perhaps "death" is just her body disappearing from Maddalena's life, but her mother's love is constant. Maddalena chose to impersonate and replace a female death row inmate, and she went to the execution ground and died. At the moment of her death, did she finally get together with her mother?

In the fourth act, Andrea collapsed in the cell and sang the aria in the play. The second aria, "Come un bel di maggio," is like a beautiful day in May. Maddalena is coming soon. Paying jailers to visit the prison, the two meet, each time with mixed feelings. They sing a touching duet of love and mutual complaints. The two encourage each other, support each other, and sing together the final long notes, together to the execution. And that's the end of the play.

Topic: "Venice Phoenix Opera House"

The opera diva, I have to memorize. "I am also the same fate as you. And I will not have effort to remind you of this same thing again."

The middle of May saw the premiere of the rehearsal of the Venice Opera House (Teatro la Fenice). I was lucky enough to listen to the live broadcast on radio station Rai 3, via the internet. It was the opera *Norma* by Vincenzo Bellini.

The Phoenix Opera House, Teatro la Fenice, caused me to remember other productions there. It is also the premier theater of my most favorite opera, Verdi's *La Traviata*.

The theater is located in Venice and can be reached by the "water bus" to the bus stop, S. Maria del Gioglio. The theater was founded in 1792. The phoenix symbolizes the immortal bird. After the fire, the theater was rebuilt in 1836 and in 1996. And the most recently one was opened in 2003. Seating can accommodate one thousand people. The theater is magnificent and beautiful. It has a classical, noble, and elegant character of opera, especially the atmosphere under the lights.

The symphony orchestra seems to accommodate twenty to thirty people, comparable to the Metropolitan Opera House in New York.

The Phoenix Theater is part of Venice's special geographical environment and waterways. Ancient Venice, as I understand it, became a maritime commercial city in 1500, located on a lagoon, with water buses in the city and special red, green, and gold wooden boats. The gondola, used as a means of transportation, has a boatman dressed in a black-and-white horizontal-striped T-shirt and black trousers. He holds the paddles in his hand, rowing with special techniques and allowing for daily tides—sometimes high tide. When the sea flows over the adjacent walkway and sidewalk, people can walk on the "passover"—*Passerelle*. Every October, the carnival begins as if it's in the tenth century. People wear makeup and masks and put on costumes to become a feature of Venice.

This special city has infinite style.

Here comes a newest news: "It was learned from the news that the European royal-blue diamond was sold for 6.7 million Swiss francs in the European Geneva auction in mid-May, 2018."

Venice enjoys sunny days. In good weather, there are Ponte Dealto links on both sides of the main canal. There are restaurants and lounges on the shore. If you have fried swordfish chops at lunch, plus cold white wine, that, along with Venice's unique style, cannot help but be fascinating.

Many facilities in Venice are related to the phoenix. The name in

Italian is Venezia, close to phoenix, and the city takes the water bus to the Teatro la Fenice. Gondola are on the waterways in the city. The phoenix, commonly known as the immortal bird, may symbolize the indomitable spirit of Venice for a thousand years. The church on the beach is like a spiritual symbol, overlooking the Adriatic Sea, close to the West La-Aegean Sea, and then to Turkey and Constantinople. Because of the special significance of the geographical position, the millennium stands still.

It is like a Western pearl, opening the channel to the Muslim countries of the Middle East, and is located in the territory of the Roman Empire of Italy, becoming a place where things and cultures gather—such a precious situation.

I cannot help but pray for the people living in the land. If it is only convenience, the location of Venice has reached its goal. Then, the residents living on this island should have experienced the exhausted feeling of "thousands of passing sails are not."

Chapter 22

Topic: "Come to Naples"

*W*ords, such as the word *invention*, appeared with the discovery of computer technology, and such a word may also appear in political and editorial articles, as well as from politicians with influential changes in social concepts.

I thought of the "The First Approach to the Legendary Novel" that I planned to write. After a while, I was confused. The opera diva and her soul were so noble and divine. After all, I would write about her life. Or was I also working on a part of the "invention."

Not only that, but I have heard that the authors of some novels already used her personal characteristics as the subject of detective novels, thriller novels, and protagonists. She is no longer an opera star but a related actress in a criminal case, and in those books, she is like an innocent victim. The accident involves some inexplicable crime cases and how to use her wits to make the mastermind behind the scenes appear and successfully come out in the story.

As for me, I am also confused. What is the basis of my writing? Is it a novel plot or a biography? If self-proclaimed as an invention, is it an offense to her?

After the "Italian Ribbon" from Milan to Rome, the opera diva went to Naples, the most important city in southern Italy and the hometown of pizza. Here also is Donizetti's opera, *Lucia di Lammermoor*, the premier city in the Teatro San Carlo. Why did she come to Naples? Did she also participate in the debut of *Lucia*? If so, her real name would be mentioned after three years from the premiere in 1838 in London, the premiere performance of actress Fanny Tacchinardi Persiani? Or was that one, which was recorded in San Carlo Opera House, performing in Naples for three years, a total of forty shows?

Schedule:
Location: Naples, Teatro San Carlo
Year and Times
1835—18 shows
1836—4 shows
1837—16 shows
1838—2 shows
(Data from Wikipedia)

Why, in the past four years, there have been different numbers of performances, and what happened to them?

Whether the opera diva can't resist the wedding tragedy of Donizetti, like the fate of Lucia and the unfortunate story in the play, is it not accepted by Naples

This creation has become one of the most important operas. Whether it is the plot or the music, it brings new inspiration to the audience and the locals. It is a famous bel canto opera and has experienced the interpretation of the leading actress. Has it overcome such a shocking theme, brought to the opera world in 1835, and its impact after nearly two hundred years?

Has the musical spirit of the opera diva been sublimated in this drama and become her famous act as the goddess of opera or diva?

And where is she now?

Topic: Searching for the emotional life
of the operatic diva from *Lucia*

With my exploration of the legendary novels and data search, the more I want to find her, psychologically, I feel the more I want to pursue her. She is getting farther and farther away from me.

I cannot write about her—her personality and personal qualities. However, some rumors and even gossip at the time began to invade my daily life through some fictional plots, rumors, and whispers. Some of these rumors have been heard, some are brewing, and some (hopefully) are irrelevant.

Back to the *Lucia* premiere of 1835, nearly two hundred years ago. The truth has no way to look around, and I can only find clues like a hint. I know the opera of the last century, perhaps based on Mafalda Favero. About Signora Favero, mentioned in the book, it is said that after winning first prize in the vocal competition and performing in Puccini's opera *La Boheme*, at the Reggio Municipale Opera in Reggio, according to speculation, she left the municipal opera house. I did not find a reliable record, however, for where she went.

Rumor has it that the opera diva came to Naples, in the southern part of Italy, on a vacation, but it is also said that she was there for the reenactment at the San Carlo Opera House, Teatro San Carlo, of her premier performance in *Lucia di Lammermoor*. The opera was first performed in 1835, premiering in Naples. It is speculated that her last performance of the opera in the last century was after 1963.

Based on the data search, I found that during 1835, the performance of *Lucia* had a peculiarity: eighteen shows in 1835, four shows in 1836, sixteen shows in 1837, and two shows in 1838. What happened to the performances in the two even years?

Going back to the opera diva of the last century, after 1963, she once again came to Naples for the drama *Lucia*. At this time, she participated in the performance at San Carlo Opera House. How would that work if the opera diva came to Naples for a vacation? She might have been out of the way, but then what happened?

She came to Naples, Italy, to participate in the rehearsal of *Lucia di Lammermoor*.

In the charming theater that was the San Carlo Opera House in Naples, the sun shone into the corridor of the theater. The chief actress of the opera recalled the past—the memory was still fresh—and felt a sense of isolation. The opera diva also felt that because this was a performance of *Lucia* that she was about to reexperience the play and everything that had happened during the rehearsal.

Donizetti's opera *Lucia di Lammermoor* is a beautiful opera that premiered on September 26, 1835. One of the characteristics of the bel canto opera is the so-called coloratura cadenza. Regarding the creation of the early baroque music section of the opera, it later influenced the bel canto music of the baroque period. Early composers such as Lully in the seventeenth century and, later, Handel created works with long phrases and no breath change, and singing the coloratura cadenza is most famous. This heavy responsibility then came to Vincenzo Bellini and Donizetti.

The story *Lucia di Lammermoor* is realistic fiction written by Walter Scott. The opera is composed of two stories that depict Lucia's family and the Ravenswood family. The story is full of suspense, surprise, and mystery.

The love story is like *Romeo and Juliet*, in that depicts the two families—Ravenswood and Lammermoor. Edgardo Ravenswood and Lucia di Lammermoor are the descendants of these two families who love each other. This is another tragic love story—they cannot be together because of their families.

When the melody opera opens, it has a dynamic bass lead singer and chorus. It establishes the foundation of the entire opera. Then, the heroine, Lucia, and her companion Alisa appear. Lucia tells her story by singing her aria, which is a two-stage melody. First, the lyrics are the main focus, and then the second stage is horse-racing songs. The position and role traits of the heroine are established, and then the hero, Edgardo, makes his entrance. He sings a love duet with Lucia that is a lyrical and tragic prelude. The first act is over.

The second act is the confrontation between Lucia's brother, Ashton, and Lucia, showing the feelings between brother and sister. The sing a duet, and finally, Ashton compromises for Lucia's happiness because of love. This is the end of the first scene of the second act.

Unexpectedly, the second scene of the second act opens with everyone cheering and singing the wedding blessing. Lucia was forced to sign a marriage contract in front of the public, and then Edgardo appears, accusing Lucia of a change of heart. This scene ends with brilliant and lively singing and a duet allegro between Lucia and Edgardo. The second scene ends in a long, high-pitched note from Lucia.

In the third scene of the second act, Lucia appears in the famous "mad scene." Among the guests, Lucia sings of the mood on the wedding night. Then everyone finds Lucia and her wedding dress covered with blood, and they see the dagger. Their performance is at the banquet, and it is also a two-stage aria, nearly twenty minutes in length, composed of many flowery phrases. Everyone is stopped by Lucia's monologue, and they slowly understand. The plot becomes clear, and scene ends in Lucia's long, high-pitched E note, which is also the highest voice of the opera heroine in the general melody of the opera. Many onlookers, seeing that goodness, fascination, and sacredness, are too weak to say anything.

Lucia's superb acting and flowery singing techniques master the atmosphere brought by the music and the feelings of the onlookers, which produced the aforementioned suspense, surprise, and mysterious atmosphere.

During the rehearsal, the opera diva had discussion with the artistic director of the theater. She could only participate in the rehearsal in the afternoon. It was to bring the music quickly to the forefront during the evening performance and also to make some secondary characters familiar with the official performance at night. These are so-called alternates or understudy actors, in general, and the opera is performed during the rehearsal in the afternoon. And sometimes, because the drama is sensational, some theatergoers will be allowed to watch the dress rehearsal. The time is ripe. When the time is up, the opera will be officially opened.

The famous chief actress of the opera was responsible for the rehearsal in the afternoon, which made the play even more sensational. The audience arrived for various reasons and relationships. They were interested in the music, and even commented on the theater for the opera.

They waited for the Lucia's mad scene, but the conductor did not want these temporary audiences to listen to the complete song. Sometimes they rehearsed in bits and pieces. Some audiences were patient and okay with that, but some of them were impatient and could not help but shout their complaints about the stopgap.

The afternoon rehearsal was finally over, and the opera diva returned to her dressing room arranged by the theater. In the room, she recalled the mad scene she'd just performed and sometimes could not help but criticize herself for one or two sentences.

Chapter 23

*I*n the tradition of the bel canto music, the notes in the melody of opera scores, in the tradition of the melody opera, sometimes must follow the singer's talent and imagination. There are many high and low voices and some small, clear, long high-pitched notes.

Lucia di Lammermoor is just one of many examples. Moreover, it can be derived, developed, and changed by the singer, and the uniqueness of the traditional vocal opera tradition is achieved.

I read three or four articles, and I thought that this period could be traced back to 1835, and it spanned between 1960 to 1970 in Italy. So far, this includes the Phoenix Opera House in Venice, Italy; La Scala Opera House in Milan; the Rome Opera House in Rome, the San Carlo Opera House in Naples in southern Italy, and some impeccable opera houses such as Reggio, Piacenza, Bologna, and Modena.

I could not help but revere the opera. I thought about my preference for opera, even as a primary school student. For more than three hundred years, across Italy, France, Germany, opera has been popular. It is obvious that the authors of these novels, essays, and special articles were more familiar with Italy; it is no wonder that they had a special feeling for Italy.

Italy is really charming.

I became immersed in the manuscripts and narratives and have been unable to return to God for a long time.

I thought of the opera, the opera world, the former studio director, and possibly the authors of these articles.

After consideration, I decided to keep these articles in my collection. I like them very much, and their content is so fascinating. Here are some reasons for this:

1. These articles are not enough to form a novel.
2. I do not know if the characters mentioned in the article, especially the heroine, the opera diva, are still alive. If so, I must pay tribute to her.
3. Who is the original author of these articles?
4. How many of the characters and places mentioned in the story are authentic?
5. Is it a historical novel? Biographical novel? Or is it just a fantasy novel?

All these mysteries and doubts have made me become more cautious.

I like opera very much and am familiar with it. On the webpage, for example, the opera star is on the Master Opera fan page, and the opera singer is there; it is not that early opera period mentioned in the article since 1835.

I think, based on the above five reasons, I will keep searching, but this also is a problem. What should I do about those who have read these articles first? Will they understand my situation? Will the readers mistakenly think that I am the writer of these articles? For example, in these articles, are the time, persons, and places mentioned my personal experiences or the retelling from a third party, or the facts I know?

Of course, I also thought that it would be up to me to take over the proposal of the "The First Approach of the Legendary Novel," and these articles were handed over to me. I am considering such a proposal and its legitimacy, and I intend to ask the boss of the studio, one of the patrons, about the feasibility.

I have to find a time to contact him and call him, I thought.

Thinking about this three-hundred-year period in modern history, from the seventeenth century to the present, I realized the opera workers have been performing and working for the opera for a long time, and the audiences can watch the opera and the inheritance of the opera. How hard it is to understand?

I thought of a recent drama series that was being staged in Milan. It is Verdi's *Requiem,* and the essence of this work appeared in my heart.

After reading these manuscripts or documents, I could barely restrain myself from the desire in my heart and the love of opera.

Looking for a chance, I contacted one of the sponsors (the boss) and asked him about this proposal. He was a bit surprised. After all, this was not an easy job. You must have an understanding of the history of opera, the background of Italy, and the environment. Some of this must refer to music materials, newspapers, magazines, even though, I had to admit, some of them had been lost.

"Let's take a look at this—the former director's research has been in the work log for this proposal for nearly a year—and then plan your work and schedule," the boss kindly proposed.

Diary: the Private Diary of the Former Studio Director

September 7

After my essay "My Opera Experience," I suddenly had an idea, Among them, I mentioned many times, "Internet viewing completes an opera performance experience," according to my viewing experience, due to the use of the internet. It takes a long time to develop a habit of using the internet, the online community, and the search engine. Therefore, I decided to define the theme of this article as "My Website Use Experience," with a subtitle of "Everything is for the opera."

My writing is with the theme of the consideration of social phenomena, making my writing based on it. I do not have the same goal and randomness as others, but it doesn't make my thoughts fall into the category of empty talk or empty content. Especially, this diary-form book is so beautiful, and I spent the price of buying a book to buy it. The inner pages of the diary have some beautiful patterns, such as the Leaning Tower of Pisa in Italy, the Arc de Triomphe in Paris, the arena in Rome, etc., reminding me of my first time traveling to Italy.

On my trip, I traveled to the south of Italy, where I could go online, send text messages, use the Line app, and listen to many great operas, all on the internet on my notebook. This is really a gift the 3C product carried. Although I stayed in southern Italy, everything was networked. In the south, the traffic is not as convenient as Rome, but everything else is as comfortable as it is in the city. In particular, the weather in the south in May, in line with the geographical environment, is like that near the seashore and the river port in the suburbs here—so comfortable and beautiful. In the meantime, because I was abroad, I had more time to use the Line app newsletter. My assistant always worried that I was on a business trip. When I was abroad, I would encounter unexpected events and send newsletters from time to time to ensure my personal safety. And I have repeatedly said, "I am very good. The locale is beautiful, and the local weather is great." Because I am traveling alone, sometimes I also hope that my assistant can talk with me more, and I often do not let her fall asleep until three in the morning here. I always cautiously contact her at seven in the evening and will not contact her as much as possible, because it would already be midnight here.

I used the internet and listened to some opera selections. In the south, during the day, I took the time to study the scores of two operas, *La Traviata* and *Rigoletto*. Sometimes I sang one or two lines, but I was still hesitant at that time, not sure if I would continue to sing. These are also recorded in the narrative of "My Opera Experience."

At noon, I went to the downstairs restaurant for lunch, a fried swordfish steak, lettuce salad, and a bottle of Sprite. After lunch, I went to the bus stop at the entrance of the hotel; it could take me to the train station. It was quite lively, and there was an ice cream shop that I would visit every time I went to train station.

After returning, I compiled "My Vocal Skills and Learning." Since I am at the stage of self-study, I have been more confident with the fragments of the opera, such as some classic arias, by listening to the CD and constantly testing the sounds. I determine what the composers want to express—their thoughts are recorded and conveyed through the scores. I, through repeated tests, understand what the composer wants to do and the ideas he conveys through the singing of the vocalist. This medium makes the audience understand the meaning of the composer and makes the work meaningful.

In addition to Facebook providing me with recent performances of the opera, there is also a website that I often use—YouTube—where I can create personal account settings, and my daily viewing preferences deepen. I can customize the homepage; it's like a personal webpage I set up for myself, and I watched some new video content that I set up, according to my preferences.

The content I often viewed is:

1. The complete opera video of the whole show
2. The entire concert video
3. Recording of an opera aria
4. Personal interview with the opera singer
5. The course of the master class of the opera singer
6. Music movies

The above videos are very rich and vivid, providing instant updates, reviews, or the life stories of these great musicians.

The films provided, if they are studied in accordance with academic conditions, can also be written in special articles, editorials, reviews, and papers. And a publishing editor who could find a publishing house that integrates music into professional books can make these musical papers turn into thoughts, ideas, and sense, and make the composers' works reborn.

September 17

I've been trying to write narratives but not for the first time. At the beginning of the millennium in 2000, I tried to write a medium-length novel, *Unfinished Dreams*. The novel tells the story of a lonely girl growing up and her work, life, and romance fantasies. She works with the music orchestra that most people yearn for. She knows a medical doctor, with whom she falls in love and goes on to marry. The story is about her life before marriage.

They met because of a free-ticket concert, and he just happened to sit next to her. In reality, such a situation might also happen to you and me. Why do they fall in love and become boyfriend and girlfriend? It is because of the perseverance of the male protagonist and the kindness of the heroine. I wrote this story so that no one doubts whether they should become lovers. Until the preparations before marriage, only the heroine's heart reveals a problem.

It is a pity that this is still an unfinished novel. Otherwise, there would be more moving plots.

In 2010, due to the studio, I began to record my life notes. In 2013, I went on a business trip to a city in southern Italy and began to write the story of *Summer Dreams*, a novel. The main reason was that I wanted to explore the age of a man who had a desire for family, marriage, and children. In my heart, I knew I couldn't linger. The beginning of the novel is about a man who is alone and his viewpoint of love and marriage, and then it's the story of his aforementioned story. The novel ends in a dream of the hero, in a meeting of the male and female protagonists, encouraging him to bravely speak out and pursue the truth, goodness, and beauty of love.

In the meantime, the collection of "My Opera Experience" tells of what I have enjoyed in the opera world in the past thirty years, to appreciate the opera, to express my love for opera, and to introduce the experience and feelings after watching the opera. I hope that the beautiful and educational significance of the opera can be conveyed to more people, so that they or lovers of the opera and classical music and even music educators will know this book. It is the mission that has been given to me.

Publishing of the books is still in negotiations, and everything is still unknown.

Since the establishment of the studio, such an environment is either suitable or unsuitable, in my assessment, but I hope that such a project of studio establishment will not be short-lived. I hope that the opera will be introduced through my articles about the opera. Traditional art can be carried forward.

How can I be fortunate enough to grow up in such a convenient environment that I can watch the opera on a TV broadcast, but at the same time be sad that the most glorious period of the opera is about to become a thing of the past?

If I could return to the era of the opera's heyday, could I answer some of my doubts through my understanding of everyday life? The style of the opera predecessors is so fascinating. At that time, it was not the best era for material, but it was the most prosperous era for opera. The opera singers mentioned in some music books and magazines contributed their time and spirits to opera and traditional art!

Below is a tribute to an opera soprano whose entire career and life I greatly respect.

Letter of thanks to the opera soprano:

> Thanks to the Italian national soprano Signora, the great singer of the opera, and for the great contribution to the traditional opera art culture. In her half-century opera performance career, she has performed her exquisite and delicate interpretation and noble and pure singing. It is the spirit of opera. Even after she retired from the stage performances, she still tirelessly promoted the younger generation and established the Baroque Bel Canto School. No one can match her for her style and character and her contribution to the art of opera.
>
> By this letter of appreciation, I would like to express my gratitude and respect to Signora.

Chapter 24

More from

Perhaps my experience was like the same national consciousness that is eager to support a great country like France. *Andrea Chenier*, a story of the opera, lingered in my mind, even after I rested and slept, and the encounter of the female protagonist, Maddalena, also was in my consciousness. Sometimes, my eyes were red and wet. When I woke up, there were tears under my eyes.

This is what I *the Private Diary of the Former Studio Director*

December 27

have to face in the coming year, and I will meet it, just like the one I wrote in a narrative, "Friends Who Have Passed Away." I could not make up my mind on whether to set aside the new position. Although I used to love it, I am sure that enjoyment is no longer there.

I am sometimes confused. Since 2009, I have become less active outdoors. I remember the beginning of the millennium, when I loved work and activities; often because of work and some social group activities, I'd join two or three places in one day, and did not think it was embarrassing.

At that time, for example, a general weekly schedule included my going to work at the company each weekday morning. At this time, my identity was that of a civil servant.

After work, on the weekend afternoons, I went to a chain of well-known fitness clubs. In fact, it was a gym sport. They were membership-based, and I was one of the members there.

At two o'clock on Saturday, I went to a church choir practice, and on Sundays, I often sang poetry in the church and participated in the whole weekend.

And back to Saturday night, I came to a studio where I planned to set up a writing room and work on the writing of the Opera Music and Education Foundation, working with music magazines and using my writing room to write a special narrative.

And now, after about twenty years and to this end of the year, I especially practiced some opera arias; for example, the aria of the final scene, with the hero, Edgardo, in the drama *Lucia*.

"Fra Poco a me ricovero."

"Tu che a Dio spiegasti l'ali."

January 13, 2018

The weather is cold; the temperature has been falling for several days, and my old problems of lower-back pain have occurred.

After an internet search, the results I obtained are not relatively specific, and the only way I can continue is to first take a rest.

February 3

It rained for nearly a week. The air felt wet, and the coldness, with such humidity, made my respiratory tract feel comfortable.

In particular, yesterday, I was walking through the hospital park behind the hospital, waiting for noontime. I found a relatively dry bench to sit on. There actually were some pigeons nearby; they occasionally screamed and walked back and forth. (Maybe it was because of the rain, but those pigeons' wings were not suitable for flying.) It felt so quiet and comfortable. It seemed like it was difficult to have leisure time.

Unfortunately, at noon, I had to leave and continue on my way.

February 16

During the winter vacation, I went to a department store.

I went to the sixth floor, saw clothing on a mannequin, and noted the lyrical style of dress. This reminded me of who?

I went to the next floor and bought the flower tea that I must drink every day, as well as fried chicken. I kept playing a game on my cell phone, and a man and woman in the neighboring seat whispered about me.

I went to the Häagen-Dazs ice cream shop and bought a scoop of ice cream.

"Today's a holiday; you could be extravagant." I heard that.

Then I went home.

February 17

I am in the studio now, suddenly remembering that I have a ticket for the concert in March, placed under the bed in my room at home in an envelope-sized folder, with some unsent envelopes.

I was thinking that if I had a colleague or a partner at work, then I could go home to get it.

However, even the students are hard to ask for this job.

I recalled an article in which I wrote, "I long for a companion and a new home."

February 23

Response to the receipt of the payment from the opera magazine, *Opera News*.

Yesterday, I finally received a copy of the opera magazine, *Opera News*, for which I submitted an article last year. I am very happy!

The manuscript was about the opera *Adriana Lecouvreur* and described the content of the opera by Francesco Cilea. The title is *"Adriana Lecouvreur* by Cilea—the Feelings of the Opera Diva."* After this article was published, there were performances in Europe (in Palermo, Italy, for example) and in the United States (Metropolitan Opera House).

I used to provide this drama on a YouTube page in late January 2018. In London, the Royal Opera House, or ROH, recorded the file on their website. I listened to the play, but I also felt strange that this play had been performed for many years, and no new recorded version had appeared. The music's aesthetic, rationale, intellect, and sensuality in the play will be performed in the new opera season of the New York Metropolitan Opera in 2018–2019.

I have repeatedly listened to the drama and watched the DVD version, which made me feel different and more aware of the drama. If that is called that "version comparison," it is too disrespectful to the protagonists of the performance; for example, the actor and singer of the opera.

After the opening of the opera and the rising of the curtain, a group of actors in the background were busy with makeup and practicing lines, until the heroine, Adriana, appeared. The stage curtain was pulled back again, and Adriana practiced the dialogue of the play. She made the viewer understand that this was the story that happened in the backstage of the theater; the actress, Adriana, is played the real-life side of the drama.

And I feel admiration for such exquisite production arrangements.

I am amazed by the European opera world, and it is performing another opera, *Andrea Chenier* by Umberto Giordano. This opera is constantly being staged, and the story of the aristocratic class is also the most popular opera of the year.

For me, if these two operas are blamed on the "jealousy" of a third party, then the two operas have found common ground, but love is still the main axis of the opera, and *Andrea Chenier* is especially fascinating. It is also because the male and female protagonists went to the execution ground and chose to die. Perhaps, therefore, the heroism is stronger than in other dramas. And in *Adriana Lecouvreur*, the heroine, Adriana, has placed her life in the stars, the whole sky with stars and the galaxy. It's as if everything was just a journey from the ground back to heaven and returning to the stars. This mood is very different, and it is very moving.

For the story of the actress, there is one more: *Alcina* by Handel. Alcina, because of a fake act with Ruggiero, made Ruggiero's fiancée dissatisfied. The story is also a love triangle. The resulting jealousy is the theme, and in the end of the drama, Ruggiero is rescued by the new lover, Bradamante, and Alcina succeeds in coming out at the end of the play.

I am so happy that I received this manuscript fee a year later. During these days, many things happened. Many new operas were staged or prepared to be staged, and I started to have new writing projects.

Everything is thanks to the care of God. I recalled that two years ago, I began to have the idea of writing opera monographs, from the first book "My Opera Experience," and the incredible establishment of the Opera Music and Education Foundation. I remembered recruiting people, looking for trusted companions, and working together for the establishment of the foundation. Perhaps the goal is still far away, but by believing in God and working together, I believe that there is still a day to achieve that goal, and the idea of loving opera will be passed down.

March 3

In the studio, I took out a company Apple iPhone and suddenly wanted to listen to a song. So I chose to listen to it from my Apple Music app's "My Favorites" collection. A good recording, a good song, is sometimes so easy and quick to listen to.

This good recording now depends on the player I am using. The voice of this vocalist, using such a player, is still fresh and sweet, still beautiful.

March 9

From the rehearsal of *Simon Boccanegra*, talking about the revival of opera in the past half century:

It is known from the opera news and the latest news that in Europe, especially in March, April, and May, the opera season will be held in Italy. First, in mid-March at the Parma Theater in Reggio, there is performance of Donizetti's *Roberto Devereux*, and in mid-April, the Bologna City Opera House in Bologna will perform Verdi's opera, *Simon Boccanegra*. In mid-May, the Phoenix Opera, Venice, will perform Vincenzo Bellini's opera *Norma*.

I calculated it myself. This kind of performance is really a bit heavy for a singer. It is measured by the physical condition and physical load of the vocalist. Such performances often were seen in some popular professional singing during the heyday of the opera field.

The works of the three composers of the opera are often used in the opera world, especially *Norma* by Bellini, and the heroic tenor is perhaps best shown in Verdi's *Simon Boccanegra* in the hero character. It needs the heroic voice of Verdi's tenor, so the character should not be too weak to be with the actress soprano, Amelia, with whom the male protagonist, the baritone, Simon, has a duet between father and daughter, with eye-catching and dramatic plots.

And for another opera, *Norma*—the first act has a trio of three protagonists, which is a love triangle until the end of act I. In the second act, mainly for the actress who plays Norma and for the male lead tenor, there are no particularly important scenes or bridge segments.

With three tenor roles, *Roberto Devereux* by Donizetti should be a special vocal tribute to Donizetti, Verdi's opera needs a heroic voice, and Bellini's *Norma* is also a melody opera. For those works, therefore, these three characters are important for the tenor, especially Gabriele in *Simon Boccanegra*.

I am very surprised. If a singer follows the schedule of the opera season, this kind of opera performance arrangement, whether it is for the opera or the opera itself and the singer of the main characters and performances of the drama, makes me recall the history of Milan in La Scala. In the mid-1950s to the early 1960s, the theater arranged five to ten different opera performances in the annual opera season. The performance of the opera house was unprecedented. At that time, the opera performances relied on some well-known performers. A prestigious vocal singer, who created a legend of the opera with her Amelia, Norma, and the depiction of countless legends is still remembered by many opera fans, as if it was yesterday.

Thanks to this generation, there is high-tech and fresh communication tools, which makes the opera performances continue to be presented to the audience in different forms. Among them, the most touching ones are these professional singers, who are learning the new roles. Their hard work and efforts have made the opera develop for more than three hundred years, since 1700. To this day, the tradition of opera art is preserved, and the meaning it gives is still long-lasting.

Soon, these plays will be performed again, and I can't help but wonder, as I listen to the recordings from opera's heyday or watch video recordings, if I will return to the theater to watch the new productions. The older opera versions have memories and nostalgia, and at the same time, the new production of the same opera in front of my eyes would bring the feeling of being in the opera world—how to stir up in my heart!

March 18

My desire to find a helper (assistant) that I can trust has not been realized.

By internet browsing, I've seen that there are posts from people who have the company's number. I just want to find a formal assistant to help me to call and contact the heads of some other units; for example, I have time to meet with the editor, conduct interviews, and take on work that I can do from here. Space, time, jump off. Otherwise, I'm a slave to work.

I also went to the Apple store to download a time-management app, a small helper like this.

However, to contact some people, even foreign units, at present, I have to rely on them.

April 9

The following sentence is an excerpt from "The Technique and Method of Pavarotti"

"As mentioned earlier, in Modena (a city in Italy, north of Bologna), there is no shortage of vocalists (including self-styled), but the only one of opera music teacher is me."

April 22

Manon Lescaut—Opera Article

Manon Lescaut, an opera by Puccini, a great opera composer in Italy, is full of romanticism, with a poetic symphony orchestra to create music, its popular songs, and descriptions. Famous female characters are as follows:

1. Mimi in *La Boheme*. This opera's work has established its international status.
2. Flora Tosca in *Tosca* is also the place where he established his position in Italy.
3. Cio-Cio San in *Madama Butterfly* is a Japanese geisha.
4. The triple drama of *Il Trittico* includes Coat, Sour Angelica, and Johnny Sigige.
5. The Chinese princess in *Turandot* tells the story of her marriage.

Manon Lescaut is classified as the first professional composition in Puccini's student days and is divided into four acts,

> The first act—a tavern in the suburbs of Paris.
> The second act—the duke's mansion.
> The third act—dawn at the port of Marseille. A large
> ship is moored, ready to transport people to New York.
> The fourth act—New Jersey in the USA.

The story is based on the novel of the same title, *Manon Lescaut*. It is the memoirs of the monks. In Puccini's opera draws on these four acts. It is quite new and challenging. His scene selection has been different from the bel canto opera, but the opera is not out of the opera tradition.

In the opening scene, with the students' chorus, the male actor, the tenor, sang the short song solo of the knight Des Grieux, and then comes the theme music and appearance of the actress soprano. But immediately because of the scream of her brother Lescaut, leaving unfinished foreshadowing after the duet of love with the male and female protagonists, the knight proposed to run away together. After that, the people found that the two persons were missing. End the first act.

At the beginning of the second act, Manon is already a lady, dressing up. She turned out to be the duke's lover but still mourns the knight Des Grieux. After a calm but choppy bridge, Manon finally starts to the embankment to sing her famous aria, "In quelle trine morbide" under the heavy curtain. Her brother Lescaut comforted her and arranged to meet the knight, after which Manon sent for the duke. Then it was the duet of Manon and Des Grieux's passionate love. Manon almost pleaded with the cavaliers to change his mind. Finally, the two got back together, and they were happy. Unexpectedly, the duke came back and bumped into the two. He ordered the guard to arrest Manon, which ends the second scene.

Intermission—this gives the audience a little breathing time.

Act III—the dock at the port, before dawn. At the beginning of the curtain, completely different theme music is presented. The composer's composition skills and technique make the viewers feel as if it's a classic film director's technique—the texture of the music, the sea waves on the dock, the moored ship. After a deep night, it is near dawn, and people awake. Like the music of the third act, Manon is about to be exiled to the United States and must say farewell to Des Grieux. Everyone regrets the fate of Manon; it's suddenly a turning point. Des Grieux comes forward and asks to board the ship and go to the New World with Manon. The climax of the story was that the captain, whether or not he agreed and after the one-second pause that was as long as the first century, said, "*Ebben, Ebben, sia.*" The victory of the finale of act III is like speaking aloud the love of two people.

At the opening of the fourth act, when the audience sees the desolate scene and the ragged clothes of the two, it was amazing that the cruelty of reality became the realism of the new creation of the romantic opera. Manon felt that she was leaving and going to death. In such a desolate, infinite desert, Des Grieux went to find water to quench her thirst. When he left, Manon had a vision and sang her second aria, "Sola, perdona, abbandonata." The male protagonist is back; Manon's nightmare has not come true. Des Grieux did not abandon her; he is back! However, Manon still lost consciousness in the desert environment.

Puccini's four-act opera *Manon Lescaut* needs to be performed by a soprano. It was once controversial and extensive in a certain time. Perhaps another composer, Massnet's creation of *Manon*, gives the audience a different impression. His Manon is light—a flowery coloratura soprano, especially in the third act. Manon's dance music, "Gavotte," gave the audience a strong and deep impression. The flowery Manon won the audience's approval. *That* is the image and character of Manon. Despite the more dramatic interpretation and performance moments in the second scene of the third act and the fourth scene of the casino banquet in this opera, the image of the coloratura is still overcome by the first impression of the audience.

Then, let's talk about the role of Manon in Puccini's *Manon Lescaut*. Similarly, the role in the story has already made the audience and listeners read this novel. The role of Manon has a preconceived impression; she may be a young girl, youthful and light-hearted, truly innocent, but she has a natural instinct, with her young and beautiful body, to capture the hearts of everyone. When Puccini wrote the play, he placed two other protagonists in the drama—her lover, the knight Des Grieux, and her brother Lescaut, with wonderful phrases in the dialogue between them. With these two main characters, the duet is to present these qualities in her nature.

The music of *Manon* is so musical, especially the bridge between the first scene with duke and the second scene, the one coloratura sung by Manon. A kind of French court-style romance is presented by scenes and music—how can people not like it? In this drama, Manon's first aria is also arranged in this scene. Manon was innocent in life, still eager, screaming for the love and enthusiasm of Knight Des Grieux to sing "In that curtain under …" How moving it is, and how exciting the plot is. All the drama is in encounters with Manon. In the second scene, the knight Des Grieux appeared, and they sing the duet of love. Manon was passionate and inspired the story, and Manon forgot everything and sang for love. In one passage, there is a high-pitched note, and after that, there is a higher treble sound. At this point in the romantic love of the two, the sentiment is sublimated, turning to the symbol of love to the "deep red rose"—thrilling. This musical theme also laid the foundation for the interlude between the second and third scenes.

In the fourth act is Manon's second aria, "Sola, perdona, abbandonata." After her self-contained appearance, now Manon is presented in a sweet, dramatic transition to the memories of the past. Manon suddenly remembers that she is in the infinite desert, and she is dying. The climax of the aria is the soprano-like treble-like dropped D, and then the final bass. Some great singers will not let go of the tail and sing a long bass note with a low-cut chorus of the drama, ending this extremely difficult aria.

Then, from the lightness of the first scene of the second act, to the second duet of the love of the knight, to the drama of the aria in the fourth act, if not for the in-depth study of the role of Manon Lescaut, how could we interpret a naive girl who becomes a mature young woman to the end, still not succumbing to her fate—the transition and change of state of mind?

The play *Manon Lescaut* will be performed at La Scala in Milan in 2019, under the command of the famous Italian conductor Maestro Riccardo Chailly.

Chapter 25

May 16

oday, I want to practice or carry out the sound practice determined by my long-planned matrix center position.

Do-me-sol-la-sol-me-do.

This kind of practice can help me, from singing such sentences, from paying attention to my own voice, to carefully listening to my own singing voice, improving the relationship between hearing and sounds.

After that, I sang the second act of Verdi's *Rigoletto*, the first scene, the aria of the Duke of Mantova:

"Parmi veder le lagrime."

I suddenly remembered that in the version of this drama I was familiar with, which has Maestro Carlo Maria Giulini as the conductor, the actor who plays Rigoletto is Maestro Piero Cappuccilli. The duke tenor is Signore Placido Domingo, and the heroine is the Romanian soprano Signora Ileana Cotrubas. And as I think of it, I first read about this CD, which was in an album shop, when I was next door to a record shop that I used to go to (now closed). At that time, I was nineteen years old. I was still studying at school and going back and forth between two cities.

This CD's full-track recording is in this newly opened record store. It's on the trip I take back to my hometown on weekends. That day, it was a holiday; maybe it was a weekend or Sunday. I often go shopping from the first record shop to the second one. It was not the first time I'd seen this opera's full recording of Verdi's *Rigoletto*, but I always hesitated for a long time. Because I was still a young teenager, I was not sure that I could accept such a realistic story. Even though I already had another opera recording, Verdi's *La Traviata*, I went to the record store for quite a long time but did not buy it.

In addition, I was in the library of the school, in the expired periodical collection area, where I read *Music and Sound* and *Music Life Magazine* and the related articles about the opera *Rigoletto* were introduced from the plot (before the CD was recorded, I already knew all the plots). I went to the anecdote about this drama.

The story is about a court jester, and a detailed introduction is given to the official title of Rigoletto. In the story of his beloved daughter Gilda's and the duke's romance, the jester is afraid that his daughter will be discovered by the duke. While hiding her in a retreat in the city, he sneaked back to the hidden place of residence and met his daughter one day. The duke, who Rigoletto did not hear, hid behind him and discovered his daughter, Gilda. It describes the feelings of the father and daughter, of the jester and the daughter, as well as the shackles of love of young girl.

I recalled my youth, and I didn't go deep into such a love story. At that time, my ideals made me not too serious about such personal feelings.

However, the music is beautifully written, and it is full of drama and dramatic tension. Moreover, the three protagonists interpret through the music, their vocal techniques, and music interpretation, making the whole drama quite enjoyable. It remains one of my favorite classical music operas, and the record company's recording technology in the golden age of 1970–1980 of CD recording makes it a classic record of opera music.

Music writing techniques—I can immediately remember all the music parts, perhaps because the opera selection that I am familiar with is also the reason I listened to it many times.

Thirty years later, I listened to the play again, went to the music bookstore to buy a score, learned to sing the episode of the show, and then learned the part. I'm still learning, trying to improve my understanding of the play and the feelings it produces.

As time goes by, I appreciate that my taste in this play is also changing.

From the worship and fanaticism of opera music to the understanding and experience of the hard work of opera production, my love for opera is still there, but the focus shifts to the hard work of making a drama. The audience appreciates it and notices. The eyes of the audience are sharp, and it is not easy to feel the production and enjoy the performance.

The beauty of the opera is its production.

June 4

Talking about some male characters in opera from the rehearsal of *La Traviata*:

In recent days, the weather has been getting hotter and hotter. I limit my time outside to avoid water loss, which causes symptoms of dehydration and exacerbates heat stroke.

M, who has a southern Italian accent. It is a bit of a vicissitude of life and a southern accent in the wind. I hope that the weather is not so hot, causing excessive dryness of the nasal cavity and oral mucosa, so that singers don't lose their voices. I also used to try to sing Edgardo, from *Lucia di Lammermoor*."

"Tombe de l'avi miei."

However, the vicissitudes of the Naples style really scared me, making me reasonably suspect it was heat stroke. The strange thing was that I didn't talk too much. During the day, I went to the studio to study in the morning, and I came back in the afternoon. I didn't talk with other people. I really don't understand why I sound tired. Maybe the reason really is the weather. I even thought I should give up practicing singing for a while and study other homework.

Alfredo is the hero of *La Traviata*. The story is based on the novel of the same title, *The Camellia Woman* by the writer Junior Zhongma. The story depicts the heroine, Violetta, wearing a camellia on her chest and attracting the attention of the leading actor. The story describes their love but they can't be together, even during Violetta's last tragedy of losing her life.

The traits of this novel are based on the subjective view of the actor, Alfredo, and the story genre described. At the same time, the novel was written in the context of the Parisian social circles at the time. In the present view, this is an old-fashioned love story, so modern people may not go to see this performed.

Giuseppe Verdi was an opera composer who objectively presented the essence of the play (this original novel). At this time, musicians and playwrights drew on the story. The highlights make the play seem to focus on a coloratura opera singer, making the novel of a past time a compact opera.

Alfredo presents a love story from a male point of view. Alfredo's character is gradual and progressive. Violetta has changed the woman's view of love because of him. At the end of the scene, even for the sacrifice of love, Alfredo, as the subjective storyteller of the novel, presents his the characteristics—young, optimistic, innocent, cheerful. But Alfredo changes from a college student, entering a master's family, to consciously encountering emotional betrayal. In the end, because of his hope and love, he seeks Violetta's understanding and talks about going to Paris together and her future life. It is full of living and humanity. Because of the interpretation of the roles, the play is really attractive, even now.

The play is not to be overstated. It is a rehearsal of the opera world. Perhaps through a traditional opera production and presentation, it can really lead the audience back to Paris in that era and encourage them to pursue their true love.

June 24

I mentioned in the proposal of "My New Year's Life Proposal" that I had entered middle age. Those who are young, relative to the elderly, may feel helpless and disappointed in the view of the average person and feel unhelpful and repulsive. However, as far as I am concerned, as I get older, I look at people who are older, and *older* is worth pondering, having in-depth discussion, and doing research.

In my world, the elderly are not just people who are inconvenient or slow-moving. They are in their psychological stage. They have many opinions and thoughts. They are different from when they were young. How do they live as a young life within themselves? Different days bring the problems they face every day. Many ideas come from their daily lives. In the morning, one person goes to the streets, one goes shopping, or one person eats soy milk and fritters in the breakfast shop. One person cooks; one person prepares lunch, takes a nap in the afternoon, or watches TV with another, so there are interpersonal relationships, social isolation, or the days when there are no chats. Many times, they may be alone.

Many of the experiences of life have turned into an indignation for them, and dissatisfaction in life has made their views on society and the world sometimes be different from the average person, which may be full of extremes, regardless of general attitude.

When I was working at a young age, I had the opportunity to contact the elderly.

Now I have stepped into middle age, and my life has changed. Slowly, I have started to live like a senior.

I used to be eager to live like a young man in his twenties and have an active social life, a circle of friends, and a life surrounded by classmates. Many valuable experiences, along with time, were gradually lost as we entered the old age, and the fast speed of that loss is sometimes unimaginable.

Sharp, mean speech sometimes is not a message that could be overcome by concern or condolences.

How long has it been since I have never spoken to an old friend? When did I last say, "How are you?" or "How have you been recently?"

Much time is spent in rushing—time on the road and the habits of our lives. This often make us ignore some details that are worthy of concern, research, and discussion. Sometimes, it is only a group phenomenon caused by people and for a long time is ignored. However, the accumulated energy is enough to make a lonely old man heartbroken, shattered like glass, and turned to irreversible damage.

All of this continues to happen, until some people forget them.

What they need more is peace.

In Verdi's opera, there is a deep description of the mood of the elderly, who are no longer young. For example, Rigoletto, the hero of the opera *Rigoletto*, was helpless and sighed about his situation. The only sustenance in his heart was that he was taking care of his daughter. By the way the aria is presented, they don't show too many personal emotions and feelings, but they concentrate on the description of the current situation and present the mood in a way that describes the current situation.

"Pari siamo! Io la lingua, egli ha pugnale." (We are all the same! I use my tongue; they use swords.)

Chapter 26

July 12

Th' here are more things in the room, more and more piles, and despite the studio, this situation makes me have to make more economic plans.

In addition, my headache is how to deal with these things. There are the following categories:

1. Clothes—winter sweaters, summer T-shirts, and warm coats, etc.
2. Paper—some expired letters
3. Books—former textbooks, new knowledge, music
4. Old sundries—old pillows, pillows, cloaks, etc.
5. Old CDs and DVDs

These are taking up space in my room, plus a big bed.

I suddenly remembered that I love to buy, so the room is full of clothes, books, and CDs I bought. If I can, I also want to find some time to clean them.

I have thought about it many times—put another shelf in the room—but it has not been implemented yet.

In the studio, I only put a desk and a floor lamp and a combination recliner. These are enough for me at the moment. I no longer take care of my appearance and my plans.

Perhaps the new life I really want is to sort and discard everything and then let it go.

July 21

I have been waiting for a long time, and finally, someone took the initiative to contact me. He provided a trustworthy contract and asked me to sign. Of course, the contract will have some attached conditions. I also asked for my needs. He agreed.

Therefore, I am renting a writing studio in an office in the city.

I posted a notice and wanted to ask a work assistant to start my project of publishing novels and books.

I have been looking forward to writing a novel about the life story of the opera diva, but I am so limited that I have no way to write it, and some of the storylines are always inexplicable to be called morality. Standardized tests—others can no longer proceed. The idea of this proposal is to describe the characters, protagonists, and the qualities of freedom in the spiritual life.

Unfortunately, it is still impossible to break through the inexplicable question in reality.

I remembered that I met one of the studio's sponsors that day, and I didn't hold too high expectations. I thought that in the position of the patron, I'd hoped that there would be works soon. However, publishing books and writing novels is only one of our partnerships. We have other projects, such as recording and making albums. And he promised he could take care of me.

When I met him, he wore a white shirt, black trousers, and black shoes. He was about two or three inches taller than me. However, when he stood talking to me, he bent down, and his conversation was gentle and courteous. There was a kind of indescribable temperament that attracted my attention.

I have repeatedly stressed the importance of trust and aid for me.

About my social problems, in his opinion, all are small things. After the talk, he agreed to make my life more secure. This is great.

A few days later, I also went out wearing a close-fitting shirt. It looked really attractive and very good. I just tried that things that attracted me. I also wore a pair of pointed black leather shoes. I got them when I first moved to the studio but never had a chance to wear them. Maybe new shoes make my feet hurt. I was on the street, thinking about what the studio needed besides stationery and some twenty-six-line notebooks, so I went to buy it.

I went to eat a lunch. I went to a noodle shop because the weather was too hot. I ate it with the green tea provided free by the noodle shop.

My postmodern life has begun.

August 17

With regard to the preparatory work required by the two units of the Opera Music and Education Foundation and the writing studio, I have reexamined the number of words written, depending on the situation, and my plan direction has become as follows:

1. Directly target.
2. Plan work-content time in schedule.
3. Find sponsors.
4. Repeat the progress on a regular basis for one month.

In this way, I can enrich the work of these two units.

At noon, I arrived at a municipal library. Since there was still some time, I took out the *Summer Dreams* manuscript and made a progress chart, such as proofreading and translation into English.

There was someone sitting next to me, but the person was temporarily out of the seat. I continued my work and didn't pay attention to her returning to her position. She opened her file, and suddenly I noticed her full table of documents, stationery, and a book. She also had notebooks, as well as colored paper labels, and a purple plastic document folder. She took out some invoices and documents to sort out. It seems that she is a writer and also held a newspaper in her hand.

Seeing the purple official document folder, I thought, *If I see that I have put together my manuscript of* Summer Dreams *and put it into a briefcase, I don't know how great it will be!*

There are one hundred original pages of manuscript of *Summer Dreams*. After finishing an abridgement, there are eighty-eight articles, plus a special article on travel themes and the part written in Rome, plus the end. The total is currently 105 articles, about 84,000 words.

This is the first draft.

The next progress plan is sorting into translated manuscripts, and I also plan to translate the second proof and third proof, in order to make the article

1. Easy to read,
2. Easy to understand,
3. Have a smooth narrative,
4. Have content coherence, and
5. Be rich in content.

Because I caught a cold, my work has been reduced recently. I can't handle too many words or sort out too much space during a working time. I expect that the first draft can be completed in early September, which should be considered fast progress.

August 22

On the way to the city and the community, I continually heard a sentence from the novel *Summer Dreams*, which may bring a little space for the community that is busy and disturbed, so that the community residents can temporarily have a rest.

I am reminded that for fourteen to eighteen years, I have stayed in the modern environment after the millennium. For such a long time, I have lived in the world of self-sufficiency, society, the city, and the world by myself, and for many reasons.

"I am just listening."

However, in daily life and in reality, no one has actually come into my life. This is what I am feeling. I have been thinking about the recruitment of people for a long time. What kind of work can I do? How long does it take? Can I continuously and confidently agree with the requirements of the job? Or will it be just a routine?

Maybe I should have asked two work-study students, different in nature—one who can work for the Opera Foundation, and one who can work for the writing studio.

Also, for my recording career, I am thinking about the title *La Musica in Camera* or *L'Aria in Camera*.

Originally, I planned to work with a radio station or a studio to record the album CD project but there is still not a suitable studio that could make classical music (they are used to sing and play rock and roll music), so I have to seek a more convenient and suitable one. For the online search, I use the words "Camera Concert," and the account is set up on the website TuneCore. This plan is more feasible. Next, there will be more new tracks.

Among them, there is a commissioned proposal, which is mainly for me, to make the opera by Offenbach *Les Conte d'Hoffmann* or *The Tales of Hoffman*. I have researched online, and there are many versions of this drama. Among them, I cite some scenes and tracks as my homework study and also will learn quickly through some audio files—for example, MP3 and MIDI files on the internet. However, with this approach, I must worry about the aftereffects, and so I must be careful.

Among the arias and choruses, there are:

1. Drinking song
2. The song of the doll
3. The final scene of the machine doll
4. Venetian boat songs (duet)
5. "Song of Antonette"
6. Antonette's final scene
7. Stella's final scene

There is one problem. For this drama—or even for many other operas—there also is a kind of drama-oriented trap. For this reason, for much opera music that I know, I still have no record. Among them, for Antonette's final scene, there is the most apparent example of the drama-oriented trap. It's unavoidable for Antonette's final scene. She still has to face this situation.

In addition to being familiar with and understanding opera music, there is another problem: this drama is a French opera. I still have to work hard to do my homework in French.

The operas I listened to this year were:

1. *L'elisir d'amore*
2. *La Traviata*
3. *Rigoletto*
4. *Lucia di Lammermoor*

The above five operas have such similar problems. In the position of an opera performer, I need more trustworthy people to be a singer; for example, I—with my body, my voice, including my speech and my singing—could preserve the essence of an opera. Otherwise, it is difficult to embody the opera music, which includes the spirit of the opera tradition.

(Here, the log is broken.)

I saw some problems after I read the notes in the diary:

1. Why didn't he continue?
2. Where did he go?
3. Where is he now?
4. Is he still alive?

After reading these work logs and during the period I have worked on it, things are becoming more and more incredible. During that period, I also inquired about some music materials. I recalled the historical documents I had read and set the time background at the end of the nineteenth century. Perhaps that is the background environment—the honor and glory of the history of Italian opera. It also includes the brewing period of neoclassicalism and modern art.

I left a letter to the sponsor of the studio. I mentioned the following in the letter:

> The translation of the narratives of *Summer Dreams* and the work of assisting publication and printing in the third place have come to an end. My work on the stage tasks has ended. Next, I am waiting for the publishing house in New York to reply. And I have already given my work to the assistant. Thank you for taking care of me."

Epilogue

I could not help but feel the excitement in my soul and in my heart, carrying my luggage and preparing to move to my destination. It was the diary of the former studio director that gave me the inspiration and idea. It was Verdi's *Rigoletto* in the 1960s. At that time, the performances in cities in Italy, such as Emilia Reggio, Bologna, and Piacenza, were over half a century ago. According to the data, I imagined that it was also the prosperous period and an environment that was conducive to the opera.

I can't wait to pick up my luggage and move toward my destination.